DISCARDED

Full Circle

OTHER NOVELS BY DAVIS BUNN INCLUDE:

Heartland
My Soul to Keep

International Thrillers
Imposter
The Lazarus Trap
Elixir

Novellas
The Book of Hours
Tidings of Comfort and Joy
The Quilt

For a complete listing of novels by Davis Bunn,
visit his website at davisbunn.com

Full Circle

DAVIS BUNN

THOMAS NELSON
Since 1798

NASHVILLE   DALLAS   MEXICO CITY   RIO DE JANEIRO   BEIJING

© 2008 by Davis Bunn

All rights reserved. No portion of this book may be reproduced, stored in a retrieval system, or transmitted in any form or by any means—electronic, mechanical, photocopy, recording, scanning, or other—except for brief quotations in critical reviews or articles, without the prior written permission of the publisher.

Published in Nashville, Tennessee, by Thomas Nelson. Thomas Nelson is a registered trademark of Thomas Nelson, Inc.

Thomas Nelson books may be purchased in bulk for educational, business, fund-raising, or sales promotional use. For information, please e-mail SpecialMarkets@ThomasNelson.com.

Publisher's Note: This novel is a work of fiction. Names, characters, places, and incidents are either products of the author's imagination or used fictitiously. All characters are fictional, and any similarity to people living or dead is purely coincidental.

Managing Editor: Natalie Hanemann
Page Design: Mandi Cofer

Library of Congress Cataloging-in-Publication Data

Bunn, T. Davis, 1952-
    Full circle / Davis Bunn.
      p. cm.
    ISBN 978-1-59554-204-5 (softcover)
      I. Title.
    PS3552.U4718F86 2008
    813'.54—dc22

2008004089

Printed in the United States of America
08 09 10 11 12 RRD 6 5 4 3 2 1

4|08
Bat

chapter 1

$\mathcal{A}$dam sat in the plush leather chair and tried hard to focus. His future depended on pushing the past aside and concentrating upon the here and now. But the contrast between these elegant surroundings and two years of yesterdays was hard to get his head around.

For the past twenty-five months, he had been imprisoned in a hard hospital chair. The previous day, he had flown from Baltimore to London. Now he was seated in a mystic realm where loudspeakers did not bark and hospital bells did not jangle and smells were not sharp as scalpels. Instead, he sat in a palace, one where the fragrance of fresh-cut flowers filled the air. A cheery fire at the reception hall's opposite end kept the English December at bay. The hardwood floors framed Persian carpets. Chandeliers marched like sparkling sentries down the high-ceilinged chamber, guarding a lovely lady behind a curved rosewood desk.

A lady who was trying very hard not to weep.

Two other women appeared through the rear doors, one bearing coffee and the other an embroidered hankie. They clustered around the receptionist.

A tall pendulum clock by the curved staircase bonged nine times. Adam had been kept waiting over an hour. Which was odd, as he had been awakened from a jet-lag stupor at seven o'clock, when a sullen woman phoned his lodgings and demanded that he present himself precisely at eight.

Time dragged at a glacial pace. Adam knew something was horribly wrong. Employees streamed through the front doors. Their dread-filled glances toward the receptionist suggested the problem was not hers alone. Whatever might be ailing this company, it approached an epidemic.

Adam reached into his blazer pocket and touched the folded note. His mother had slipped it to him as he had left the hospital. The single sheet had been opened so often the creases were tearing. Illness had reduced his mother's handwriting to a scrawl. But the words were clear enough. *The sign will signify many things. Gifts, and the chance to use them to the fullest. Purpose, and the joy of doing well for yourself and others. Hope, and the illumination this brings to your every day. And love. When you arrive at your destination, I pray you will know clearly that you are doing the right thing. Love, Mom.*

Adam rose from his seat, turned his back to the receptionist, and stared at the art adorning the walls. A collection of framed black-and-white photographs rimmed the reception chamber. Adam knew most of them intimately, as they were by his mother's favorite photographer. He stepped forward until he saw his reflection in the glass. A sign, his mother had written.

"Mr. Wright?" A heavyset young woman with a funereal expression paraded down the broad, curved staircase. "I'm

Robin Oakes. We spoke this morning. Mr. Dobbins will see you now."

"I was told to report to Mr. Austin."

The woman was halted in the process of starting back up the stairs. She chose her words with care. "Joshua Dobbins is the company's chief financial officer."

"Mr. Austin isn't here?"

"Please, Mr. Wright. Joshua Dobbins does not like to be kept waiting."

The broad stairs ended in an elegant hall where polished oak doors stood recessed within carved frames. They passed two clusters of people sharing muted conversation and grave expressions. More strident than the company's somber mood was the artwork on the walls. The line of Eve Arnold prints clawed at Adam, slowing his progress.

"In here, if you please." The woman knocked on the hallway's last door. "Mr. Wright for you, sir."

"Come in, Wright. That will be all, Mrs. Oakes."

Adam stepped into the office and halted before yet another Eve Arnold print, one that held a special poignancy. The office was high-ceilinged with plaster scrollwork around the chandelier. A pale silk carpet rested upon the polished wood floor. Between him and the desk stood a marble fireplace. The desk was rimmed by tall bay windows.

"Come sit down, Wright."

"I'm fine where I am."

"I didn't ask for your sentiments. Come over here and take a seat."

The man behind the desk was made a silhouette by sunlight. For two years Adam had faced cameras he couldn't see because of the surrounding spotlights. He showed the man a professional calm he did not feel. "You're going to fire me, right? So get it over with."

The man responded with a double-beat of hesitation. "What makes you say that?"

"Your secretary told me Mr. Austin was not in. Your chairman personally offered me the job, and he's my only contact with your company. Your secretary said you are the finance director. You're probably the man who must approve all new hirings. And by the scene I've been watching downstairs, I'd say your company is in serious crisis."

There was only silence from the other end of the room.

Adam went on, "You ordered me here at eight so you could get rid of me before the boss arrived. But then you made me wait for over an hour. I'm thinking you decided to check with him, but he wasn't reachable. Now you've either argued your case, or you've decided to take matters into your own hands. It's doubtful Austin would make an issue over his number two firing a low-level peon. Especially when your company has been hit by incoming fire and is hemorrhaging badly."

"What have you heard about our company's problems?"

"Nothing, until this very minute."

The man, who rose from his desk, held one shoulder slightly lower than the other, or perhaps it was merely the result of his ill-fitting dark suit. A narrow tie was offset by a starched white shirt. His features were pockmarked, his mouth a thin slit. He was a man made to wield the corporate dagger, and without remorse.

"Come sit down, Mr. Wright. No, over here. Will you take coffee?"

"Will I be here that long?"

"I'll take that as a yes." Joshua Dobbins settled into the sofa and waved Adam into the suede chair opposite him. He phoned for coffee, then replied, "I won't deny it, Mr. Wright. I had intended to dismiss you out of hand."

Adam caught the slight inflection. "And you still might."

Mud-gray eyes flashed with something that might have been humor. "This ability of yours to read subtle signs is impressive."

"I'm an analyst," Adam replied. "A good one."

"Are you indeed?" A moment's further inspection, then Dobbins asked, "That print on my wall, the one you noticed upon entering. No, don't turn around. What can you tell me about it?"

"The photograph was taken by Eve Arnold."

"We are hosting a retrospective of her work. You might have read the plaque downstairs. Anything else?"

Adam saw no need to explain how a copy of that very photograph had adorned his mother's studio. "Eve Arnold shot the picture in 1963, on her first trip to England. She was over to do the promo stills for a movie version of *Becket*. Richard Burton played the starring role. The photo was taken of his death scene. The photograph shows Elizabeth Taylor off camera with their three children. Their daughter was terrified, watching her father die. Eve Arnold took the photo just as Taylor cradled the child in her arms and explained that Burton was acting. The child refused to leave the set until she saw her father get up again, Burton's death was that real."

A curious secretary laid out bone china and poured coffee. "Be so kind as to bring me this gentleman's file from my desk, Mrs. Oakes. Help yourself to cream, Mr. Wright." Dobbins accepted the file from his secretary, read for a time, then said, "There is very little here to commend you for a position with our company."

The morning's initial shock was wearing off, leaving Adam hollow. "Those pages don't include why Mr. Austin spent two days with me in Washington."

Adam had met the chairman of Oxford Ventures, a boutique investment house, at a conference in Washington. Oxford Ventures handled about half a billion dollars, mostly from Oxford college endowments. They were also involved in spin-off companies based upon research done within the university system. Peter Austin had started the firm sixteen years earlier. Oxford Ventures was moderately successful, a steady but not spectacular earner. Over the past five years, returns averaged about fourteen percent. They were known to take the long-term approach. Adam knew this because he had checked. He knew a great deal more besides.

Dobbins slapped the file shut and tossed it on the table. "So tell me what the file does not say, Mr. Wright. Such as, why you chose not to complete your university studies. You left after your second year, I believe."

"My third."

"We have two Americans on our staff, both graduates of Ivy League schools."

"Did either of them double their investment capital their first year in the market?"

Dobbins was saved from responding by his secretary appearing once more. "Sorry to disturb you, sir. But this can't wait." She walked over and handed her boss a note.

He glanced at the slip and said, "The file is on my desk. You were saying, Mr. Wright?"

"One of my business courses required us to set up and run an investment portfolio. I did it with real capital."

"Your family gave you the funds?"

"My family had no funds to give me."

"Yet you had free capital with which to invest." When Adam did not rise to the challenge, Dobbins went on, "Any number of young men and women manage investment portfolios while remaining in school."

"That was not possible in my case."

The gaze sharpened. "How *did* you obtain your funds?"

"I'd rather not say."

"I did not ask for your preferences. My objective is to detect sordid little details before they might risk the company's good name."

Dobbins' secretary glanced over. Her somber expression was broken by a tight little smirk. There was no question in Adam's mind. She knew.

"I'm waiting, Mr. Wright."

"I got an acting job."

"Acting? As on the stage?"

"I was doing some amateur work with the university's theatrical society. Before."

Dobbins flipped the pages of Adam's file. "You had a partial scholarship to Georgetown?"

"Full academic." Adam focused on the secretary's smirk and continued, "A Hollywood studio began shooting a prime-time drama based on the Washington political scene. They came to the college looking for somebody they could cast as a congressional intern. I got the part."

Dobbins recalled they were not alone. He looked over to his secretary. "Are you quite done?"

"Sorry, sir. I can't seem to find the file."

Dobbins rose and walked over. "So you quit university to act on television, and you invested your capital in your spare time. Not what one might call stellar qualifications."

"I gave Mr. Austin a copy of my investment records. I tripled my money in six years."

Dobbins impatiently sifted through the papers on his desk. His tone was not cold so much as impersonal. "Then why do you need to work for us, Mr. Wright?"

"I lost my money in a personal matter."

"Personal, as in an investment gone sour, perhaps?"

Adam sighed. There was nothing he could say that would change the man's mind.

Dobbins said to his secretary, "Go ask Trevor if he took the file and failed to inform me."

"Yes, sir." As she turned to leave, Dobbins' phone rang. The secretary picked it up. "Mr. Dobbins' office. Oh, good morning, sir. Yes, he's right here." She handed him the phone. "It's Mr. Austin."

"I've been trying to reach you. Yes, he's still here. No, I'm sorry, I do not . . . Peter, I must ask that you hear me out . . . Yes. Very well. If you insist."

Dobbins set down the phone. He studied Adam for a long moment. "You have thirty days, Mr. Wright. One month to come up with a pair of investments our firm would otherwise not have identified. And not one instant longer."

chapter 2

*K*ayla was awakened far too early by the ringing of the phone. Her flight from Tanzania had been delayed six hours, and it was after midnight when she finally arrived home. She had then taken her first true bath in months, reveling in such marvels as clean water and a spotlessly tiled bath and lights that worked. When she had emerged, her father had gone to bed. She had made a midnight snack of toast and marmalade and drank in the home's silence.

Thankfully, her father's new wife of nine months was not around. Kayla had only met the woman once. That time, their argument had brought the restaurant to a standstill. The next day, Kayla had left to resume her work in Africa. If the excuse of urgent work had not existed, Kayla would have invented one.

As she rose from bed, the phone rang again and finally cut off. Her parents had started attending morning chapel the winter her mother had become ill. Her father still attended almost every morning. Peter Austin never took calls before church. It was one of their home's ironclad rules. Kayla made herself a cup of coffee, then returned upstairs to dress. When she came back downstairs, Peter Austin had returned from church and stood reading the *Financial Times* at the kitchen counter. He set down his coffee, kissed her forehead, and examined Kayla's dark suit. "I told you on the way back from the airport. The board will not be able to speak with you today."

"If I could just have five minutes—"

"Kayla." He addressed the paper instead of his only daughter. "There is no money for you."

"We don't need much." Kayla had spent much of the night rehearsing the words she intended to use before the board. She had never thought it would be necessary to use them with her own father. "Without the extra funds, we face bankruptcy before Christmas."

Peter Austin sighed and turned the page. Sipped his coffee. Shook his head. Sighed again.

"The robbery shouldn't mean the ruin of a very good project. The welfare of over a thousand families in Kenya and Tanzania hangs in the balance."

"No one denies the value of your work. But none of this matters in the face of our current—"

"You know it matters, Daddy. Three minutes. Please."

Nineteen months earlier, Kayla Austin had returned from working with England's largest private aid organization with a plan. One that had sparked a passion and a drive in her that had astonished everyone, most especially her father. Together they had presented her plan to the company's board: set up a trust to run this project, and use the resulting publicity to promote the company's good name. The board had agreed, with one proviso. Kayla was sent back to Africa with instructions to hire a number two with solid business experience.

Everything had proceeded swimmingly, until the business manager had vanished. With all their capital. He had stripped the project's bank accounts and even robbed the office cash box. But the money was not all he had stolen. By then, Kayla had become engaged to the man she was certain was her life's mate.

All of it gone in an instant. Grinding her heart into dust.

Kayla swallowed against the rising gorge. She hated speaking the man's name. "Geoffrey robbed us blind."

"That was ten months ago. Now is not the time—"

"Now is *precisely* the time. We've almost managed to make a go of it. That's why I came back now. To show just how close we are. We've scaled back and revamped and we're *so close*. All we need is the money to see us through this crisis."

Her father turned to look out the rear windows. Something in his demeanor left Kayla certain he was no longer listening.

Peter Austin had a caesar's profile. At nearly sixty he still possessed a full head of silver-white hair. His eyes were deep-set beneath a strong ledge of a forehead. A melodious voice balanced the strength, revealing the man's calmer side. The openness. The ability to care very deeply. Kayla noticed the subtle changes she had missed the previous evening. His eyes were ringed by sleepless worry. The skin over his cheeks looked like aged parchment. "Are you all right, Daddy?"

"Kayla, this is highly confidential." He closed and folded his paper, then slowly stroked his tie. Deliberate actions, intended to add emphasis to his words. "Our company is in serious trouble."

"I don't understand."

"No. Of course you don't. What is far more disturbing, neither do I."

She followed him out of the kitchen and into the front foyer. "I need to do this, Daddy."

"You are far too dark from your time spent in the sun and much too thin. And this morning you resemble your mother to an impossible degree." Peter Austin buttoned his jacket and pulled the lapels down tight, the financial warrior preparing his armor. "Let me phone Joshua and I'll meet you in the car."

Oxford Ventures, Peter Austin's company, was located in a sprawling Summertown manor that Kayla's mother had rescued from ruin. Amanda Austin had found the manor while pushing her baby daughter around Oxford in a pram. Summertown was the city's Victorian quarter, started in 1850 when university dons were finally permitted to marry and move out of their college quarters. Until then, professors had followed the medieval practice of remaining single until their teaching days were over. Following the change and continuing until the First World War, the dons filled what had previously been farmland with stately redbrick homes.

As Peter Austin turned onto Oxford's Ring Road, he said,

"I'm having lunch with a new man. An odd sort. You might like him."

"Am I only attracted to odd men, Daddy?"

Her father did not rise to the bait. "My phone call just caught Joshua in the process of firing him. I suspect that battle is not yet over. Perhaps you'd care to join us for lunch?"

It was hardly a ringing endorsement, as far as Kayla was concerned. "It's hard to think beyond the board meeting just now."

"All right, daughter."

"Besides which, I have an endless list of things I can't find in Dar es Salaam, all of which we desperately need."

"Must you be leaving again soon?"

"I have to, Daddy. You know that." But she did not want to add to her father's woes, particularly not before the board meeting. "So tell me about this new man. What is his name?"

"Adam Wright." Peter Austin turned through the arched stone entrance. Sunlight lanced through the parade of winter-bare elms and speckled the drive. "I met him at a conference in Washington. I was so taken with him that I skipped most of why I made the trip and then offered him a job. Joshua was livid."

This was unlike her father. While her mother had filled Kayla's young years with her various passions, Peter Austin was a rock. He took a measured approach to all of life, while her mother became swept up in one enthusiasm after another.

The wind shoved at Kayla as she climbed from the car. The cold slipped through her coat and struck at her very bones. As they walked the gravel drive, she saw that her father's face once again bore a grave expression. The two of them were lost in very different mental universes. Kayla asked quietly, "Do you miss Mother?"

Peter Austin blinked slowly. "What a question."

"Do you?"

"Every day." He climbed the front stairs behind her. As the front door opened on its electronic hinge, he added, "Which makes your being away so very difficult."

Kayla entered the reception hall and froze.

The walls displayed a collection of Eve Arnold prints.

Peter Austin stood and watched his daughter take a slow circuit of the room. She stopped by the placard explaining that the photographs were part of a display of Magnum Photos, on loan from the Tate Gallery. Kayla stopped before one of Marilyn Monroe and said, "I remember this one."

"Of course you do. It was your mother's favorite."

A signed reproduction had hung in her mother's dressing room. Eve Arnold's photographs had been another of her mother's many passions.

Peter Austin said quietly, "You are more like her than you will ever know."

Kayla understood him completely. "I couldn't possibly stay here in England, Daddy."

"We could be very happy, you know."

"My work is there."

Kayla found herself recalling something from the year her mother died. One of those small items easily forgotten, and so piercing to remember. Kayla had been standing outside her mother's hospital room and overheard Amanda Austin tell her husband how he never looked more handsome than when he smiled through his sorrow."

Peter Austin smiled at her in just that way. "I am very proud of all you have accomplished, Daughter."

Kayla took a nervous breath. "Let's hope the board feels the same way."

chapter 3

"M om? Hi. It's me."

"Oh, my. Is it Sunday already?"

"No. Thursday." Adam's top-floor office had formerly housed four junior analysts. The other three desks were now empty. The long narrow room was brightened with skylights and furnished in flowing Swedish lines but remained a far cry from the executive quarters two floors below. "How are you?"

"Adam, you know what we decided." His mother's voice was soft but relatively strong. Eleven o'clock in Oxford was six in the morning, Maryland time. His mother had always been an early riser. Nowadays, this was her clearest hour. "You agreed it was best if we spoke once each week."

"Only because I didn't want to leave after another argument."

"You have to be strong, son."

He did not want to hear her go through all the reasons for his being four thousand miles away from her bedside. So he changed the subject with, "Mom, I got the job."

"Well, of course you did."

"This place is in serious trouble. I don't know what's wrong yet. But I'm thinking major meltdown."

"So they need you even more than you expected."

"The way things look, I might be home pretty soon."

"Did you find anything that might be the sign we spoke of?"

"Maybe. The entire building is filled with Eve Arnold prints."

The sound from the other end of the line was so alien, Adam feared his mother was choking. "Mom?"

"Eve Arnold? Really?"

Adam realized she was laughing. He tried to remember the last time he had heard the sound. "They're holding a retrospective. They've got Marilyn's picture, you know the one, she's leaning against Clark Gable's car from *The Misfits*. It's downstairs in the reception hall."

"That was always my favorite."

"How did you know? I mean, about the sign."

Adam expected her to respond with one of her standard edicts, as in, A life without faith is only half lived. Or, Blindness of the heart can be cured with one small act. Words he had been ignoring for years.

Today, however, she said, "The veil between heaven and earth seems to be diminishing. From time to time, there are the most astonishing moments of crystal clarity. I can see the door ahead, and it is wide open. Angels pass through and speak with me."

He set an elbow on the table and leaned his forehead upon

his fist. She had never spoken openly of this before. Even so, after twenty-five months of crises, he should have been ready.

His mother went on, "There is a glory in suffering. I wish the lessons had come in some different form. But they haven't. At least for me." Her breathing rasped across the distance. "This is why I asked you not to call but once a week, son. We knew it would be a trying time. But we also knew this was the right move."

"You did."

"No, Adam. No. We both knew this. You have seen me through the impossible. You have had your own trial by fire. You must be strong now. Find a future without hospitals and suffering. For both of us."

"I need to be there with you."

"You are. Now I want you to do something else for me. Find another old lady who faces her own trial. Give her a reason to smile."

"I'll try."

"I'm very proud of you, son. Call me Sunday."

Kayla had been granted three minutes with the board. She needed only two. Their gazes were rifle barrels that shot down her words before they were fully formed. But what truly silenced her was her father's demeanor. Peter Austin, her strongest ally and constant support, stared blankly at the conference table. His bearing matched his suit, dark and gray and all the life starched out. Nothing he might have said could have impacted her more.

Kayla was reduced to proper formality. She apologized for having lost the company's capital. She apologized for having hired a charming thief. She neglected to mention she had done so only because they had insisted upon her bringing in a business manager. She apologized for delaying her return. She had hoped her team could pull things together and survive. They almost did. Kayla passed around details of their current financial situation, which showed clearly that a relatively small injection of further capital would bridge them into success.

She then left the boardroom. Her unspoken request dangled in the air like a spinning target, waiting to be shot down. Kayla could almost smell the gunpowder as she shut the conference room door. Not one of the board members had even glanced at her handout.

She took a slow tour of the building, ostensibly to examine the Arnold prints. In truth, they merely gave her something to look at while she moved about. She had never imagined the board would turn her down flat. She had expected a severe dressing-down and a check reluctantly written for a fraction of what she needed. Even that would have granted her the chance to work out terms with their African bankers. But to receive nothing was unthinkable. Kayla walked the halls, surrounded by her mother's soft presence, and tried to breathe around the gaping wound. Nearly two years of struggle. All her hopes. Gone.

She was midway along the upstairs hallway when the change finally struck home. She could hear a man struggle through a phone conversation because that was the only sound. Normally the building's top floor possessed a sort of joyful pandemonium. Her father's junior employees played like human skyrockets, their frenetic excitement a force that infected the entire building. But not today. Kayla found herself drawn toward the open door. She saw a young man hunched over his desk, his forehead planted upon his fist. His accent was American. She heard that he spoke with his mother. The conversation was clearly tearing him apart. Finally he hung up the phone, took a hard breath, and used both hands to drag his hair from his face. Kayla retreated unseen.

She carried the young man's distress back downstairs. She realized the same anxiety was reflected in almost every face she passed. Oxford Ventures had always been a special place, full of her father's vibrant optimism and power. Normally, the air was electric with potential. The company's reputation among the business community was legendary. Peter Austin did not merely invest other people's money. He made things happen.

Kayla retreated into a little alcove just outside her father's private office. When Kayla had been twelve, and her mother's pending departure had filled their home with shadows, her father had fitted this out as her little niche. An eighteenth-century wormwood writing desk, just twenty inches wide, had been positioned against one wall. Peter Austin had bought her a Victorian occasional chair with scrolled arms and extra padding in the seat. Her father had then presented Kayla with her very own key to his private filing system and showed her how the bottom drawer with its polished mahogany front had her name in the little brass frame. The drawer was hers to stow whatever she wished, and no one, not even he, would dare touch a thing. They had never mentioned the reason for these gifts. Nor why the secretaries had gathered in the doorway and smiled at her. Nor why everyone in the company gave her such a warm welcome whenever she arrived.

Mrs. Drummond, her father's secretary, an unflappable woman who had been with Peter Austin for nineteen years, gave Kayla her customary greeting of a solemn nod. As though Kayla had been in the day before and not absent for almost a year. Mrs. Drummond possessed little ability for familiarity.

Slipping into her alcove and seating herself at the desk brought Kayla no relief. The bulletin board above her desk was filled with work from her last visit home—financial projections and spreadsheets and photographs, all of which had been packed into the glossy brochure she had produced for her investors.

All lies.

She was still seated when her father returned from the boardroom. "A rather curious thing."

"What, Daddy?"

"This young gentleman I was telling you about. He seems to have caught Joshua unawares." He knocked gently upon the side-wall, another gesture from their past. Even in the most frantic of days, he would tap the wall as he passed, just letting her know he was there for her. "I have the distinct impression Joshua was not altogether sorry I insisted we give Adam a chance."

This was so like her father. At the worst moments of their life together, when the entire world seemed blanketed by shadows, her father would search out something good to share with his daughter. Kayla was flooded with memories of other such times. "I'm so sorry, Daddy."

He gave his distinct smile, warm and sad and loving, despite the world falling apart around him. "Mrs. Drummond, ask the young man to join me."

chapter 4

*T*he Eve Arnold prints followed Adam back down to the chairman's office. His mother once described Arnold as a simple woman who used her camera to reveal the humanity behind the gloss. Adam had often thought the description applied equally well to his mother. But Eve Arnold had been granted an impossible chance and used it to fly straight to the stars. There the similarity ended.

The chairman's suite occupied what once had been a pair of south-facing lounges. The secretary greeted him with, "Please go straight in, Mr. Wright."

"Thank you." The prints were here as well. Behind the secretary's desk hung the famous shot of John Hurt, used as a cover of *Life* magazine. His mother had kept the same shot in her darkroom.

Which was why Adam almost missed the striking young lady seated in a narrow alcove. Adam's first thought was that she was being punished for something terrible. She had to be. She possessed the saddest eyes Adam had ever seen.

"Do come in, Mr. Wright," said Peter Austin.

But what Adam wanted was to walk over and tell her he would make it better. Which was ridiculous, of course. Adam had far too much experience at being caught in the snare of helplessness.

As he entered the office, the chairman asked, "Will you take coffee?"

"Thanks, I had some upstairs."

"With Joshua? Did you indeed."

The chairman's inner sanctum occupied a corner lounge. Bay windows illuminated two walls. The office was rimmed by oak wainscoting. Above the panels hung another series of photographs, only these were not part of the Eve Arnold collection. They were recent and in color.

Peter Austin stopped in the process of shutting the door, watching as Adam approached the closest picture. "You know this view?"

Adam responded with a nod.

"Please take a seat. You have traveled to Africa, Mr. Wright?"

"Other than one failed trip to Hollywood, I've never been anywhere."

"Yes, you mentioned that journey when we last met." Peter Austin settled into the chair across from him. "Be so kind as to tell me what you see in the photograph, Mr. Wright."

"Mount Kilimanjaro," Adam replied. "This was shot from the Tanzanian side. Probably on the road leading from the airport to the capital."

"How very remarkable. And you say you've never . . ." The chairman turned at a soft knock on his open door. "Kayla, do please join us. Let me introduce you to Adam Wright."

Kayla spared him one more glance before walking over to the same spot where Adam had just stood. Then she turned and gave the room's other photographs a slow and careful sweep.

Adam drank in the sight of her. She did not belong here. No matter how nicely dressed she might be today, she was alien to this world. Her features were deeply tanned. Her short hair was Arabian black, silken and dark and laced with copper highlights. She was a desert cat, a lynx who spared little attention for her appearance.

Peter Austin said, "For the past two and a half years, my daughter has directed a relief project headquartered in Dar es Salaam. She sent me these photographs but has never seen them here before."

Kayla turned back and said, "Shame on you, Daddy."

Only when the chairman smiled at his daughter did Adam realize how much the man had aged since their meeting in Washington. Peter Austin replied, "You leave us for over a year, my dear, you are bound to come home to a few surprises."

Her father's old Mercedes was so quiet Kayla could hear the clock ticking. Peter Austin had been involved in a bad accident before Kayla was born. As a result, he rarely drove except to and from the office. The boxy Mercedes was eleven years older than Kayla and had been driven less than twenty thousand miles. It was not so much a car as a vessel for memories. Kayla leaned against the headrest and recalled her mother doing the same thing. Amanda Austin liked to pull her shoes off and prop her stockinged toes on the dash. It seemed to Kayla that she could still smell her mother's perfume imbedded in the old leather.

Kayla could feel the cold radiating off the window beside her face. The late-afternoon sky was shod in a light as pale as childhood fables. The lands held to an emerald cast, the hills soft and woolly as the sheep dotting the pastures. Kayla's mind saw not one landscape, but two. Overlaid upon the stone-lined roads and quiet hamlets was a harsh realm of ocher dust and barefoot children and donkeys plodding under impossible loads.

Peter turned off the main road onto the narrow lane leading to their village. "What did you think of my new employee?"

Kayla shut her eyes. The young man's face was instantly there before her. "He's quite handsome."

"He's done some acting," Peter Austin replied. "The odd amateur gig at university. Then he was cast into a minor role on some drama. He referred to it as a nighttime soap."

"Why did he give it up?"

"It was more the other way around. His character was caught in bed with a congressman's wife, and shot. Afterward he went out to Hollywood and made the rounds. But apparently there are a thousand such handsome young men seeking each new role. He hated the experience. And then a personal crisis took him back to Washington."

Kayla admitted, "He reminded me of Geoffrey."

"The thief in Tanzania? How so?"

"I don't know. They look a little alike, but it was more than that. I can't quite put my finger on it."

Peter gunned the motor up the final rise and entered their village. "I am thinking of personally mentoring him."

Kayla looked over. Her father had never before had a protégé. "How do you know you can trust anything he's told you? Did you have him investigated?"

Peter turned through the gates and drove past the church. "Joshua asked me the very same thing. We've completed a cursory background check. I also had Mrs. Drummond talk with his references. All of which were glowing." Peter Austin pulled the keys from the ignition and toyed with them like worry beads. "I had to cancel our lunch because of this ongoing crisis. Adam is joining us for an early dinner. You can ask your own questions and make your own decisions."

"Daddy, please. I only have a few days home. I don't care to spend them . . ."

He raised a hand to silence her. The keys dangled from his thumb. "Kayla, there is something else that must be discussed now. Honor is pregnant."

If he had reached over and slapped her, the shock could not have been greater. "Daddy, you're sixty years old."

"Fifty-nine, actually. And in my trade, precision with numbers carries great significance."

Through the tumble of conflicting emotions, only one comment emerged fully formed. "Is that why Honor has been away?"

"She wanted me to have time to tell you, yes." Peter Austin

gripped Kayla's seatback and shifted closer. His face was as solemn and strained as she had ever seen. "Kayla, I want you to listen very carefully. Your happiness has always been one of my greatest concerns. But we are enduring desperate trials and I need your support. You will make peace with my wife. And you *will* join us for dinner."

chapter 5

The world was shaded by a velvety dusk as Adam left Oxford and headed west into the Cotswold Hills. Adam's day had remained dominated by a sharp sense of detachment. Few people spoke with him. The company was locked in morose anxiety. He had begun his search for new investment prospects, yet could not shake off the conversation with his mother. The company car passed through fields shaded flaxen and rust and pearl. Trees still clutched a few autumn-flamed leaves. Towering elms stood sentinel about ancient farmhouses and herds of sheep. Hamlets were timeless works of art. Rosebushes grew high as young trees and clung to many houses. Time had decreed the homes and vines must join as one, for the branches ran like brown limbs about windows and doors and eaves. Between the tiny villages, stone walls and hedgerows moved in to clutch the road.

They turned onto a smaller lane that ran along the base of a valley. Adam pointed at the river rushing alongside the road and asked, "Does it have a name?"

"That's the Avon, sir. One of many. A thousand years back, give or take a century, every Cotswold village with a decent stream laid claim to the Avon. The courts tried to sort it out back before the last war. Didn't get far. Problem is, the river splits so often round these parts, they might as well name the rain in the sky." The driver was a ruddy-faced man with a walrus mustache and seen-it-all eyes. "But that's England for you, sir. We'd argue over the song a kettle sings, given half a chance."

They entered a village signposted as Hawthorne. They climbed a hill, the road a tunnel beneath flanking oaks. The peace was strong enough for village children to play an intent game of soccer in the middle of the street. "Here we are, sir. Hawthorne House."

The house and the neighboring church were built of daub and wattle, with crossbeams hewn in a time when trees were not expected to grow straight. Both had newer additions of honey-colored stone, which had obviously been cut by hand, for the chisel marks were very evident. The house was almost as high as the church and shaped like a barn. Metal braces attached to cross-ties kept the walls from bowing more than they already did. The roofs of both structures were of slate so old the lichen grew in a rainbow of grays.

Peter, his wife, and his daughter came out to greet him. Peter Austin's wife was a beauty in her mid-thirties with a distinctly English complexion, not so much pale as delicately colored. Honor was dressed in linen slacks of autumn copper with a matching sweater that revealed her growing belly. She held her husband's hand through the greetings, saying little, but saying it with genuine warmth. Kayla's greeting was a subdued hello that matched Adam's own internal state.

The home's interior was a remarkable contrast of the ancient and the new. The original barnlike structure was one room almost fifty feet long, segmented by hints of walls and broad single stairs. The front and rear of the house contained broad windows. The dining area grew by the north wall, the kitchen by the south. This meant all three rooms were illuminated by the setting sun. The living room contained slender-limbed furniture of suede and flowing wood colored to match the walls. An open balcony lowered the ceiling above the kitchen. The kitchen was rimmed by a counter and framed by spotlights. Adam felt ever more the stranger, a product of crisis and strain that had no place in this warm haven.

Kayla had experienced a recurring dream during the lonely time surrounding her mother's final illness. Not lonely in the sense of not having friends or a loving father. But Kayla and her mother had known a very special relationship, and Amanda's death had left a gaping wound in her thirteen-year-old daughter's life. Around that time, Kayla dreamed she moved to a different universe, one where her mother had never left. When she awoke from these dreams, she lay in bed for hours, the blankets up high enough to block out every hint of light. She relived the dream over and over, skipping downstairs and hearing her mother singing in the kitchen, and everything back the way it should have been.

There was certainly nothing about the young man seated

across from her to explain why she should think of the dream now, for the first time in years. Adam Wright followed the conversation with a smile that only heightened the sorrow in his eyes. He said little but listened well, drawing the home's story from her father and Honor.

The house and the neighboring church were two of the oldest structures in a very ancient region, both dating from the late tenth century. Medieval life in this region, Peter Austin explained, was dominated by two forces, wool and the church. At one time, the church had owned all the surrounding land. Their home had been the village tithe barn, erected inside the church wall so thieves would be discouraged by the unspoken threat of stealing from God. The practice of serfs tithing to the church was lost when Henry the Eighth broke from Rome and distributed all the church's lands to his loyal followers.

"The barn was a ruin," Peter Austin said. "My first wife, Kayla's mother, found this wreck of a house the year after I started my company. I could hardly afford to buy a place that would take three years to rebuild."

"Five." Kayla spoke for the first time since they had seated themselves at the table. "It took five years."

"Of course it did." Peter smiled at the memory, his weary strain easing momentarily. "My first wife sold a farm she had inherited, some stocks, and all her jewelry except her grandmother's broach and her wedding ring."

When Honor rose and began gathering plates, Adam asked, "Are you sure I can't help with anything?"

"Next time. Tonight you must play the honored guest."

Peter Austin said to his wife, "Adam was very taken with your photographs of Mount Kilimanjaro."

"Actually, the photographs are Kayla's." Honor began carving a roast of lamb. "I had a professional studio enlarge and frame them as a present for Peter. He missed Kayla so, especially now with the company going through such trials."

Peter interrupted with, "We won't discuss that tonight."

Kayla saw how Adam had intended to do just that, only to subside with his questions unspoken.

Honor went on, "I thought it might draw Kayla a bit closer, if you could be reminded of the reason why she was absent."

"They're beautiful," Adam said. "Truly."

Kayla looked down at her empty plate. Learning that the photographs had been Honor's gift heightened her sense of disconnect. Kayla listened to her father and his new wife moving about in the kitchen. She did not need to lift her head to know she would see a couple moving about their home with the ease of genuine love. The facts were inescapable. She should never have come home.

Adam asked very softly, "Are you all right?"

She looked up. Adam was watching her with an intensity that and left her feeling very exposed. "Why shouldn't I be?"

He kept his voice so low that the pair in the kitchen could not hear. "I don't mean to pry. You just . . ."

"What?"

"You look like I feel."

The words draped themselves over her heart. Impossible

that she could feel such sudden tenderness toward a man she did not know. "How did you know about the pictures?"

"The Arnold prints, or the ones in your father's office?"

"Both."

"My mother was a photographer. Eve Arnold was her favorite professional. I grew up around those pictures."

"And Dar es Salaam?"

"My mother has been very ill. About eighteen months ago, she got so much better we thought maybe the worst was behind us. She's always wanted to go to Africa. It was her dream. So I gave it to her."

"And you couldn't go?"

"Mom didn't have health insurance. By then my finances were in pretty awful shape. I got her into one of those package tours to Mount Kilimanjaro. She didn't try the climb, of course. But she had a wonderful time."

Honor had joined them by the table. "I'm sure it meant the world to her."

When the evening closed, the farewells were said and the guest smoothly dispatched. Kayla joined Peter and Honor on the front step and watched the company car depart in a quiet swirl of polished speed.

Honor said to the star-flecked night, "What an utterly astonishing young man."

Peter turned to his wife. "Why do you say that?"

"When I know, I will tell you." Honor stared at the empty forecourt. "In some way I can't quite explain, he reminds me of you."

Kayla shivered against more than the uncommon cold and wrapped her arms more tightly about herself. She studied the two of them, a couple in love and sharing a world where she was merely a guest.

Honor said, "I like him. Very much, in fact."

"I'm so pleased to hear you say that."

"I'd like to see more of him, Peter."

"That can be arranged." He stroked her face.

Kayla mumbled a good night and reentered the house. As she climbed the stairs to her bedroom, she was struck by two thoughts, both equally hard to absorb. The first was, her father had found the home life she had yearned for in her dreams. Not once, but twice.

The second was, she was a guest in this home only because she herself had made it so.

chapter 6

*B*efore she arrived home, Kayla had imagined she would sleep forever. The past several months had been so stressful, and the heat so awful, she had scarcely managed more than a few hours' rest each night. Yet here she was, back in her big bed, in her room of stone and light and timbers, awake to early bird-song and the day's first church bells.

Kayla had forgotten how loud the bells could be. After a few days the bells would fade into the background. In Africa, when she remembered home the bells never sounded a single note. Yet now they rang so loudly they might as well have been in the bed with her.

When the ringing ended, Kayla heard the soft scrunch of footsteps, the quiet murmur of morning voices. She rose from her bed and went to her window. The family bedrooms occupied the upstairs of the stone wing. Downstairs was her father's home office and a room set aside for business meetings. Wisteria flamed in autumn colors about Kayla's bedroom window. She could feel the day's chill radiating through the glass. Kayla saw her father and Honor standing in the forecourt, talking with a cluster of other villagers who attended morning prayers. Honor held her husband's hand with both of hers. She watched Peter with an expression of deep concern.

Kayla dressed and went downstairs to find coffee waiting. She tried to begin a list of tasks she needed to complete before returning to Africa. But the board's denial left her feeling drained. She took her coffee over to the rear doors and stared out over the mist-clad valley until the phone rang.

A familiar voice said, "Good morning, Kayla. Welcome back."

"Hello, Joshua." Kayla did not share her father's affection for the company's number two. Joshua Dobbins was perhaps the coldest man she had ever met. But Joshua's central goal in life was to protect her father, which made them natural allies.

Joshua asked, "How are you?"

Kayla replied, "Oh, I think you know."

"Yes. I'm sorry. Will you be returning to your Africa project?"

She forced herself to smile as Peter and Honor came through the front door. Her father looked as though he had not slept. Kayla replied, "To the last wretched day."

"You are indeed your father's daughter. Is Peter back from church?"

"He's just coming in now."

Peter tromped slowly down the front hall, kissed his daughter's cheek, accepted the phone, and said, "Yes, Joshua. What is it?"

Honor motioned her into the kitchen. "I need to ask your advice. Your father's birthday is in seven days. He says the photographs in his office are the only present he needs. But I want to give him something to . . ."

"Make him happy." The proper answer was instantly clear. "Make him do something to get his mind off the company. A weekend at Claridge's and a night at the opera. He went with Momma when I was five or six. They talked about it for years."

Up close, Honor's eyes were made to melt a man's heart. "Will you still be here for that?"

"I'll leave the day after his birthday. I have to."

Here they were, the two of them standing by the coffee-maker, talking like normal people. Instead of a daughter who celebrated her father's third marriage by remaining in a dusty compound three thousand miles to the south. Kayla expected Honor to protest over her missing another Christmas. Instead, Honor said, "I'm so worried about him."

"Daddy looks very tired."

"He's exhausted. But more than that. He's lost a good deal of his old fire. And confidence." Abruptly Honor reached forward and enfolded Kayla in an embrace so tight Kayla felt the woman's belly press hard against her own. Kayla clung to her, not from affection, but rather because she needed a moment to crush yet another wave of regret. When they released each other and Honor pressed her palms to the corners of her eyes, Kayla wondered which woman was the stronger, the one who controlled her tears or the one who let herself cry.

The handset chirped when Peter set it back in the charger. The two women stepped into the hallway together and found Peter standing by the narrow entry table, frowning at the sidewall.

"Is everything all right?"

"If only." Peter reached into his jacket pocket and extracted a slip of paper. He held it out to his daughter. "It's not what you need, darling. But it's all we can manage just now."

Kayla accepted it with numb fingers. She felt Honor's hand rise up to touch her back. The check was for fifty thousand pounds. It was drawn upon her father's personal account.

"I wish it were more," her father said.

Once again Kayla fought against tears. "Thank you, Daddy. So much."

Four months. That was what the check meant. Four more months to find a long-term solution. From where she stood, four months was an eternity. Deliberately she refolded the check and put it into her pocket. Kayla looked up. "Is there any way I could help out around the company?"

"There won't be any more money. You'll be wasting your time."

"It isn't that, Daddy. When I was thirteen you found me a job. You helped me then. I'd like to help you now."

"You were a godsend." Peter studied his daughter thoughtfully. "As a matter of fact, there is something perhaps only you can do."

In preparing for his new job, Adam had checked the rental agency websites and been staggered by the cost of housing. Furnished apartments in Oxford cost more than in Manhattan. He then looked through the university's website and found a page titled "Accommodations." On it was an ad that read, "Central leafy north Oxford, single rooms for quiet academics, excellent rates for the right people." When Adam called, a woman with a harried tone turned him down flat. Only academics might apply, she announced. Graduate students or postdocs or lecturers only.

Adam asked, "Do you know any place I might be able to find a room?"

"Where is your job?"

"I'm not sure." He started leafing through the papers piled on his desk, searching for Peter Austin's card.

"Young man, I can hardly assist you without that information. After all, Oxford is not some picturesque little village."

"Here it is. Oxford Ventures is located in Summertown."

The woman went silent, then, "You're coming over to work for Oxford Ventures?"

"Is there a problem?"

"Kindly wait one moment, please."

Adam sat and listened to the call's cost tick skyward with the seconds. Then a reedy voice said, "I would have thought Oxford Ventures would be paying its American employees sufficiently well that they would be seeking riverside flats, not furnished rooms."

The voice reminded him of his mother's, aged beyond years by an ailment that robbed the voice of tone as well as strength. "All this has happened so fast, I'm not sure how much I'm actually going to be paid."

"Always know the figures, young man. That is the second rule of life. Would you care to tell me what is the first?"

He started to say no. Then hesitated.

"I'm waiting."

"Have a moral compass that sets your course."

"How very remarkable."

"That's what my mother would say," Adam confessed.

"Well, well. Honesty in this day and age. And from a young man who listens to his elders. Might I inquire, who is your contact at Oxford Ventures?"

"Peter Austin."

"Yes, I can see how one might be tempted to move on trust and seek answers later. Very well, young man. Being an American gentleman, I assume you are rather overlarge."

At six four and a hundred and ninety pounds, Adam assumed he should reply, "Definitely."

She had a chuckle like dry stalks rubbing together. "Then a chamber under the eaves would hardly suffice. Tell Mrs. Brandt I said to give you one of the garden rooms."

The morning after his dinner at the Austin residence, Adam lingered over his coffee, pretending to read a paper discarded by one of the academics. The house was a massive redbrick pile, with the upper floors given over to paying guests. Of the family who had once lived here, only the widow was left, though apparently her children and grandchildren came through every weekend. All the other residents did biomedical research in the labs that were a short walk away. The residents referred to the widow as Professor Beachley and spoke of her in awe. Over their

communal breakfasts, Adam learned the widow and her late husband had formerly been leaders of the Oxford scientific establishment. Adam had spoken to her only once since his arrival, a brief
hello. The old woman had been pleasant enough, crouched over
her walker as she had maneuvered from her front sitting room to
her back bedroom. Adam had been given a middle-floor room
with tall ceilings and a view over the unkempt rear gardens.

They breakfasted around the oval dining room table, fed
by Mrs. Brandt, the same housekeeper who set out clean sheets
twice weekly and collected rent. Breakfast was at seven thirty.
Anyone who was not seated on time could still have coffee and
make their own toast, but there would be no cooked breakfast
and nothing whatsoever if they arrived more than twenty minutes late. Mrs. Brandt had quite a number of such rules and
used them as a means of keeping her charges in their place.

Adam turned with the others at the sounds emanating from
the front hallway. A young woman emerged from the professor's
study, sniffling into a handkerchief and struggling for control.
"Thank you for seeing me, Professor."

"My dear, let Mrs. Brandt fix you a cup of tea."

"I have to get to the labs." She glanced at her reflection in
the hall mirror. "I look an utter wreck."

The professor accompanied the young woman to the front
door, leaning heavily upon a cane. "Remember what I have told
you. You face not one problem, but two. The first is scientific
in nature, the second intensely personal. And no one, my dear,
can aid you with the external issue unless you first learn the
essential lesson of *trust*."

The woman remained blind to the circle of young scientists who watched her from the dining room. "No one can help us. It's too late."

"Only if you insist upon making it so."

She reached for the door. "I should never have come."

The professor sighed her farewell, shook her head, and thumped back into the front room. Only when the parlor door shut behind her did the breakfast murmurs begin once more.

"Excuse me, Mr. Wright." Even the housekeeper was subdued by what they had all witnessed. "You are wanted on the telephone."

He followed Mrs. Brandt back to the kitchen. "This is Adam."

"Hi, it's Kayla. Daddy has asked me to take you into Oxford this morning." She spoke with careful formality, as though reading unfamiliar words. "I hope that's all right."

"What about my work?"

"I'll explain that when we meet. Where are you?"

"Number eighteen, Norham Gardens Road."

"I have to stop by the office first, so I'll see you in about an hour."

When Adam hung up the phone, Mrs. Brandt noted, "Whoever that was, she certainly managed to wind your smile muscles up a notch."

He found no reason to store his grin away. "That," he announced, "was the boss's daughter."

"Can't be bad." Mrs. Brandt dried the morning dishes and stowed them away. "Is she attractive?"

"Very."

"Rich, pretty, and phoning you your second morning in the country. My dear departed mother would say the pair of you were risking a hefty fine for speeding."

"Sounds like a smart lady."

"Oh, there were no flies on my mam."

Adam thought of his own mother and recalled her words from the previous afternoon. Find an old woman in need, she had said. Give her a heart's desire, or something like that. Adam asked, "Could I speak with the professor?"

"After that last little incident, I should think she'd like nothing better. Wait one tick, and you can take her in a fresh cup of tea."

Twice on their way into town, Kayla almost told her father that she'd rather not do the task he had set for her. Both times that Kayla started to speak, her father received phone calls. He wore a headset that she had never seen before. All she could hear was his responses, which were both terse and harsh. Kayla's protest died unspoken.

She had never seen her father like this before. Nor had she heard this voice, as though he spoke around wet gravel. The second time he punched the button to end the call, he breathed hard, as though he had run a race. "What's the matter, Daddy?"

"Joshua."

"Your number two. The man who has been with you since the beginning."

"Joshua is not often wrong. But he is now. Spectacularly, indisputably, wretchedly wrong." They passed through the big front gates and drove down the graveled drive.

Kayla followed him toward the office. The morning light was strong, the sky clear, the cold so strong it slipped through her three layers and gripped her bones.

Peter stopped on the top step and declared, "You are an elixir to an impossible time, Kayla. I know you had your own desolate reasons for coming home. But right now, in this minute, I consider your presence a genuine blessing."

When they entered the foyer, they found Peter's secretary standing behind the reception desk with Joshua's secretary and another lady. "Oh, good morning, sir. Mr. Dobbins asked to be informed immediately upon your arrival."

Peter handed Kayla the car keys and said, "Perhaps you should wait here. Mrs. Drummond, come with me, please."

Joshua's secretary, Robin Oakes, possessed a ravenous craw for gossip. As soon as the chairman disappeared, her attention returned to whatever was masked by the reception desk's overhang. "Soon as I spotted his photo in the file, I knew I'd seen him before. My daughter downloaded this photo off an old fan website."

Kayla stepped forward, away from the cold radiating off the glass doors as the receptionist replied, "He looks even better in the flesh."

"I never did care much for the show itself," Robin Oakes

went on. "All backstabbing and nastiness and folks messing about where they shouldn't."

The receptionist said, "I remember the critics dubbed it '*Dallas* by the Potomac.'"

Robin Oakes smiled at the unseen page. "Our bloke played some staffer with the unlikely name of Blade."

Kayla stepped around the desk. "Can I see?"

Robin Oakes stepped to one side. "It's amazing what you can find on the Internet these days."

Adam Wright looked ready to step laughing and mocking from the page. The force of the photograph was riveting. Above him blared the headline "Coming to the BBC, the show the critics love to hate, *Washington Affairs*." Adam stood in a standard male model pose, hands on hips, twisted at the waist so that his entire upper body formed an arrogant angle. He wore a flashy suit and an expression that hit Kayla very hard indeed.

The similarity to her African thief, the man who had stolen her money and dreams and heart, was staggering.

The resemblance was not so much physical as in attitude. Oh, they both had dark copper-blond hair and a handsome strength to their features. Both were tall and wide shouldered and narrow waisted. But Adam's eyes were a rich brown, while Geoffrey's eyes were green. And Adam's chin was not as deeply cleft, nor his nose as sharp. And his lips . . .

The receptionist asked, "You've met him, have you?"

Kayla blinked. "Adam came for dinner last night."

"What was he like?" the receptionist probed.

"Fine. I mean, he was over for dinner with Daddy."

Her gaze was drawn back to the photograph. Adam mocked them. His arrogance was total. He did not sneer so much as simply not care. And this was what reminded Kayla so much of her former fiancé. Not who Adam was. What he had the potential of being.

Her thief of a lover had never exposed his true nature. Geoffrey's quick charm, his flashing wit, his ability to smile through the worst they had faced in Tanzania, all this had blinded her to the truth. Until the morning Kayla had arrived in the office and discovered everything she had known about him was a myth. Over the months that had followed, a different image had taken form. One where his smile mocked and his words lied. Just like the man in this photograph.

Kayla's mental vision shifted from the memory to the man. Not the photograph. Who Adam was *now*. Because one thing she was totally certain of was, this picture was not the Adam Wright she had met the day before. Something had drastically changed this man.

"And you just happened to be there to dine with them, did you," Robin Oakes said.

"He's gotten under your skin already," the receptionist said.

"Don't be absurd."

"Then why are you scarlet as a Christmas ribbon?"

She was saved from needing to respond by Mrs. Drummond's returning. She handed Kayla a slim envelope and said, "Your father asked me to give you this, Ms. Austin. Along with his thanks for helping out today."

Kayla left the company, slipped behind the Mercedes' wheel, and carried the mental image of Adam's photo with her into town. That and the mystery of what had stripped Adam of the arrogance and the strength and the carefree haughtiness of a pirate.

chapter 7

There was absolutely no reason why she and Adam couldn't be friends, Kayla told herself repeatedly as she walked the tree-shrouded sidewalk to the last house on Norham Gardens Road. The brick Victorian home was neither a wreck nor a monstrosity, but it had the potential to become both. A vast assortment of bicycles were dumped in the weed-infested front garden. The portico was almost lost to an invasion of ivy, and the roses growing up the side wall had clamped thorny fingers all the way to the roof. The windowsills wept dry white tears.

The woman who answered the door was brisk in the manner of one long used to saying no. "Can I help?"

"I'm here to collect Adam Wright."

"Which would make you Mrs. Austin."

"It's Miss, actually. How did—"

"Of course it is, how silly of me." She pushed open the door. "This way."

The housekeeper walked to the door of the front parlor and knocked. "Miss Austin is here, Professor."

"How delightful. Do please show her in."

Adam stood by the parlor's fireplace as she entered. He gave her his fractured smile in greeting. "Come have a look at Dr. Beachley's family."

The room held a very genteel clutter. A sterling silver tea set was also home to a dozen tiny Smurf dolls. An antique ivory sailing vessel anchored a stack of infant's picture books. A gold card-box held marbles. A children's puzzle covered a priceless French Imperial side table. Books were piled on chairs, on tables, on mantels and shelves. They formed pillars beside the fireplace and the doors. "There are twenty-seven in this picture," Adam said. "Her children and grandchildren and two great-grandchildren."

A tiny old woman was almost lost in a high-backed chair by the front windows. The sunlight made it difficult to see her clearly. "The photograph you are admiring was taken in the master's garden at Christ Church. Christ Church is the largest of the Oxford colleges, endowed by Henry the Eighth. My husband and I were both tutors there. Do you know that term, tutor?"

"Probably not the way you mean it."

"The tutorial system is drawn from the dawn of Western civilization, when students met alone with a teacher who guided their study. It is the portion of my work at Oxford which I miss most. Sparking the latent hunger in an active young mind."

Kayla turned from the picture. There was something about the voice, or perhaps the manner of delivery. A woman from a distant past, asking gentle questions that probed deeply. The old woman continued, "Lewis Carroll was also a tutor at our college. His young niece used to come and play with the master's Cheshire cat. Which is how the story of Alice and the world beneath the tree came to be written."

"I remember you," Kayla said softly. "You're Professor Beachley."

The old woman smiled. "As do I remember you, my dear Kayla. I recall fine warm summer afternoons, not all that long ago, when another young lady came to play in that very same garden. Your mother was one of my favorite students, which was odd in a sense, as biomedicine was just one of her hobbies."

"Passions," Kayla corrected.

"Quite right. Hobby is much too faint a word for how immersed your mother became in her interests." She waved at Adam. "Be so kind as to draw another chair over for your young lady."

"Sure thing."

"Thanks, but we really need to be going."

"You resemble your mother to an astonishing degree. Though whether she ever had a suntan quite like yours is questionable. Where have you been?"

"Tanzania."

"Working on your own store of passions, no doubt." The professor's gaze tracked back to the picture above the mantel. "We are actually twenty-nine now. My husband is gone, and I'm still rather cross with him for leaving me here alone. But I've since gained another two grandchildren and a third great-grandchild, and I do so enjoy their company. If only the hours between their visits did not drag so." Her keen gaze returned to her two visitors. "I don't know what I would do without these visits from my paying guests. Are you quite certain you can't join me for tea?"

"Another time."

"I shall look forward greatly to that occasion, my dear Kayla. I find such pleasure these days in seeing the past come alive again. In the meanwhile, would you pass on my best to your father?"

"Of course."

"A most remarkable gentleman, Peter Austin." She smiled at Adam but directed her words at Kayla. "Be good enough to say that I heartily approve of his new young man."

"What was that all about?"

Adam shut the front door and followed Kayla down the walk. The morning sky had become veiled in clouds light as winter's first frost. A bird chirped defiantly against the chill. "I was about to ask you the same thing."

"You first."

"Do you want the long version or the short one?"

"We'll walk into town and you can regale me the whole way."

"What about work?"

"Daddy asked me to do this with you."

"Are you warm enough?"

"No, but the walk will help."

"I remember when Mom got back from Africa, she couldn't

get warm for weeks." He unfurled the scarf from around his neck and handed it over.

"What about you?"

"I've never been bothered much by the cold. Why do you sound so American one moment and English the next?"

"The proper term is cross-cultural." Kayla led him to the end of the road and down a path that connected to the first set of university playing fields. "My parents both came from America. They met while studying at Oxford and never left. My mother did not want me to grow up sounding totally British. When I was twelve she sent me back to the States to her own private school. I hated being away from my parents. After one term Mother let me come home. But she made me promise to return to America for university."

"Then she died. Your mother, I mean."

"When I was thirteen."

"Did you go back?"

"Yes. To Amherst." Kayla resisted the urge to press for an answer to her original question. Either he would talk, or she was wrong in her estimation. She had certainly been wrong about men before.

Adam said, "My mom has been having dreams. At first, I pretended that they were just the result of her meds. She's on megadoses of some really heavy stuff. But she's also very religious. No. I take that back. She hates it when I call her religious. She says religion can get in the way of what's important. Don't ask me what that means. I've spent my entire life blocking her out whenever she gets going on that subject."

He jammed his hands deep into his pockets. "You still want the long version?"

Kayla had an uncommon urge to reach over and slide her arm around his. Entwine herself in close. Feel his strength and his heat as he spoke. It was a ridiculous urge and swiftly repressed. But the thought was strong enough to raise a flush to her cheeks. "Go on."

But he didn't. Adam scuffed his feet along the paved walk, ignoring the neighboring rugby match, even when the players came roaring up within a stone's throw of their path. His breath puffed toward his feet as he finally said, "I'd like to say it doesn't matter. That the whole thing is just one woman coping with the impossible. But I've been trying to be very honest about all this. Mom really prizes honesty, and I haven't given her much of that in my life. I guess that's why I was a decent actor. So I decided that was what I would give her here at the end. Honesty. I'm getting all tangled up here, aren't I?"

Kayla said softly, "The dreams."

"I *feel* them. She tells me these things, and I'd love to just shrug them off and give her a hug and walk away. From her and what she's saying and everything that's so totally out of control. But if I'm going to be honest, then I have to admit that when she talks about them, I feel like I've got this huge bell inside me, and it just goes *bong*." He made two fists and shook them. "Mom's last dream was that when I got here, I'd find a sign that she was right to tell me to come and I was right to do what she asked."

"You didn't want to come to England?"

"Are you kidding? Mom is *dying*." The word chopped his breathing into tight fragments. "I *hated* the idea. But she begged. I hated that even worse."

"Why did she ask you?"

"She said I would have to discover that for myself."

"You found the sign, though, didn't you." Kayla remembered the conversation she had overheard between Adam and his mother. "The Eve Arnold prints."

"You can't imagine what it was like walking in and seeing those images from my childhood all over the office walls."

"Actually, I can."

Adam did not seem to hear her. "I talked with Mom yesterday. She said to find another lonely old woman. I don't know if it was from a dream or not. But the words resonated like the other times. So I did it."

"Your visit with Dr. Beachley," Kayla said.

"I'm taking her to some church service at her old college tonight. I forget what it's called. The last service before the students go home for Christmas."

"Advent," Kayla supplied. "It's a very special occasion, the high point of the school's winter calendar."

"You should have seen her face when I offered." Adam looked so sad. He might have been talking about the professor, but his thoughts were clearly on another old woman, one much farther away. "Dr. Beachley used to go with her son, but he's been relocated to Edinburgh. The rest of her family are either too far away or busy with kids."

This time Kayla did not resist the urge. She took hold of

his arm, moved in close, and said, "You just come with me before we both freeze to the spot."

She took him to her mother's favorite café. For the students who used it daily, the place was just another cramped café set down just another narrow cobblestone lane. The air was filled with end-of-term chatter and steam from the old-fashioned cappuccino machine. Everything was done by hand. The ceiling was so low Adam could not stand upright. The tables were rickety and piled with students' bags and scarves and hats and mittens. The benches were the same as when Kayla had come as a little girl.

The man behind the counter resembled the ruddy-faced gentleman who had served her long ago, and the concoction was still made in the time-honored fashion. Chocolate was scooped from a tin bearing the crest of the company that had imported chocolate for eleven generations of English kings. He used a reed whisk to whip the liquid to froth. The shop became filled with the perfume of the Spice Islands and redolent with the memories of a mother who used such moments to describe the voyage their chocolate had made. Devonshire cream and Channel Islands milk were steamed to perfection. Tall glasses with wire frames were filled two-thirds with chocolate, then topped with an inch of creamy foam.

Kayla had not been in the shop since the last time her mother took her. It was just too painful to come alone. To ask her father would have meant explaining, and that would only have opened his old wounds as well as her own. Kayla paid the man, then carried the glasses back to Adam's corner table.

Light through the lead-paned window turned his hair both russet and gold. Adam looked like the perennial graduate student, one whose stipend had long since run out. His hair fell over his ears and his frayed shirt collar. His navy jacket was substandard, especially for someone who worked for her father's firm.

Kayla seated herself across from him. "Drink."

He did as she ordered. He blinked and licked the froth from his upper lip. Drank again. "Wow."

"You like it?"

He took a deeper swallow. "What *is* this?"

The same deep welling came over her, such that she reached across and took his hand. Just friends, she reminded herself. Because that was all it could ever be. She had no heart left to give to a man. Especially a complete stranger. The words fluttered and rustled through her brain like autumn leaves in winter's first wind. Just friends.

Adam looked down at her hand holding his. He set down his glass. "Did I say something right?"

"My mother brought me here. Long after she graduated, she kept coming back to visit friends who had once taught her."

"Like Dr. Beachley."

"Especially her. I haven't seen the professor since the funeral. Or come back here."

She watched him finish his drink and sigh his satisfaction.

"You have foam all over you. Chin, nose, mouth, cheek. You drink like a little boy."

He liberally applied his napkin. "Better?"

"Much." She slipped the envelope from her pocket and slipped it across the table. "I'm an official company emissary today. I asked Daddy if I could help out with something. This was it."

Adam made no move toward the unsealed envelope. "Does this have something to do with why I'm not in the office today?"

"Sort of. Open the envelope, Adam."

He did so, pulled out the single slip of paper, and stared at it dumbly. "Five thousand dollars?"

"Pounds," she corrected. "About ten thousand dollars at today's exchange rate."

"For what?"

"He said you were to consider it a signing bonus."

"But I haven't. Signed anything, I mean. We haven't even agreed on my salary."

Kayla released his hand. "You've said it yourself, your mother's illness stripped the cupboard bare. You're living in rented rooms. Your clothes, how can I put this?"

"I'm not after charity."

"Joshua wants to fire half the remaining staff, starting with you. Daddy calls it a gradual amputation and has refused. This morning, Joshua told my father that he intends to take the matter up with the board. He says that either they make these severe cutbacks, or the company goes under."

"What does your father say?"

"It's three weeks to Christmas. What difference does it make if they wait until January? That's what he told Joshua. What he told Honor . . ."

"Go on, Kayla."

"He didn't actually say it. But what he's thinking is, the company is going under."

"How long does he think they have?"

"Three months at the current level of employment."

"So three months if he keeps the people, and how long if Joshua gets his way?"

"Twice that, maybe a bit more."

"That's a big difference."

"These aren't just employees to Daddy. They are *friends*. They share his *vision*."

Adam looked at her with an intensity that seemed to peel away the layers. "You are a really great daughter."

"I don't feel like it at all. I feel . . ." She pointed at the check. "Daddy says you should have a bonus for coming all this way. As chief financial officer, Joshua has to sign off on all employment contracts. If Joshua gets his way with the board and you're fired, Daddy might not be able to give you anything then."

"It's been a while since I've had extra money." Adam picked up the check, shook his head over the amount, folded it carefully, and stowed it in his pocket. "Are we done?"

"No. Daddy intends for you to spend what days you have as his protégé. He needs you to look like one." She rose to her feet and said briskly, "Let's go kit you out."

chapter 8

*T*hey left the café and entered Oxford's old town. Adam felt himself transported to a distant era, one where gargoyles might well spread their stony wings and leap from high gables. Kayla led him down cobblestone lanes, tight caverns carved from buildings of stained glass and golden stone. Occasionally the crowds pushed them together, causing their bodies to brush. Adam wondered if she shared the same electric hum every time they touched.

Kayla named ancient structures with the casual manner of introducing old friends. The Radcliffe Camera, Foyles, Brasenose, Magdalen, Balliol. She spoke of others who had walked there before—Isaac Newton, C. S. Lewis, Cromwell, Tolkien, a dozen kings of England, hundreds of heads of state from all around the globe. She walked him through the Covered Market, past displays of pheasants nailed to the butchers' doorposts by their tail feathers, and pig trotters stuffed with smoked bacon, and forest mushrooms pickled in dark ale. Adam emerged at the other end and was blinded by the sun, such that all his senses were filled with light and the scent of Kayla's hair.

Relationships had never come easy to him. His connections to women were shallow. Yet here, in a world removed from any he had known, at a time when everything in his life was either shattered or uncertain, Adam found himself unwinding. The prospect of deepening mysteries beckoned within the sunlit lanes.

He drew her to one side and declared, "I want to help."

"What?"

"You. Your father. The company. I want to be part of solving this crisis."

"There might be nothing anyone can do."

"Still, Kayla, I'd like to try."

She nodded thoughtfully and slipped her hand around his arm. "You make me feel a little ashamed."

"Why?"

"Daddy gave me a check this morning. Fifty thousand pounds from his own savings. It's to help me try and sort through the mess we're facing in Africa." Their walk was slower now, but purposeful. Adam let her guide him to the door of a barbershop. "All I could think of was, four months. This gives me four more months to find a way out. And here you are, broke, a stranger, four thousand miles from home, maybe no job in a week's time, and you want to help."

The bell over the door jangled as they entered. Kayla put his name on the list, then guided him to the waiting area. When they were seated, Adam leaned in very close and said, "Give me the money."

"What?"

"Fifty thousand pounds gives you four months, that's what you said. So take twelve and a half for the next month and let me invest the rest. I'll set you up a couple of investments that feed your project a regular income."

"You have no idea what you're asking."

"I'm trying to give your project some extra breathing space."

Kayla shook her head so vehemently it carried through her entire body. "You don't know what you're asking," she repeated.

"I know your father's gone to bat for me. A stranger he has no reason to trust. Especially when his firm is facing something pretty awful. Okay. So I owe him big-time. And he's concerned enough about what you're doing in Tanzania that he's covered his walls with your photographs." Adam leaned in closer still. "I'm good at what I do, Kayla. Very, very good."

After the barber, Kayla first led him to the bank the company used. Once the check had been cashed and an account opened, she guided him next door for a new cell phone. From there Kayla led him along yet another pedestrian lane of cobblestones and growing shadows. She stopped before a shop whose bowed window was framed in wood blackened by time. The gold lettering above the door declared it to be as a haberdashery and gentlemen's clothier, established in 1608. She asked, "Are you comfortable with spending money?"

"I haven't had much experience lately."

The door gave a cheerful ring as she pushed it open. "Do yourself a favor and don't look at any price in here."

The haberdashery was narrow but very deep. When Kayla introduced herself and explained what they were after, they were led to the rearmost room, one that most customers never saw. The shop's back chamber was fitted out like a gentleman's club. The walls were oiled panels, the wood's grain lost to candle smoke and age. Kayla settled into a horsehair settee and watched as the salesman treated Adam with a butler's deference. At her insistence, he purchased a suit shaded somewhere between navy and smoke, a jacket, two pairs of slacks, three dress shirts, two ties, and an overcoat. Adam did as she had instructed, biting down on his worries over the cost. Only once did he look at a price tag. It was enough for a quiet cry of very real pain.

For Kayla, time became split into tiny fragments. The day's every nuance could be extracted and examined. She saw the dust motes dance in light from the narrow rear windows. She tasted the waxy oil used on the wall panels. The salesman whistled a rambling tune as he pinned Adam's trousers. Kayla recalled playing with her dolls on the same ancient Persian carpet while her mother sat in the chair where she was now, talking with her father as the salesman stood him upon the same stool that Adam used.

Kayla had always assumed she would grow up and find a man just like her father. She had thought the pimply-faced young men of school would one day vanish, and in their stead would be her prince. Then it was university in America, and young men with brash voices who spoke of the money they would earn or the power they would wield, and how Kayla would fit so beautifully into their futures. Ambition was their calling card. Their intelligent gazes and strong features and easy confidence proclaimed that they had been born to claim the future.

Her last year at school, Kayla had begun fearing that her chance at any true passion had been whispered on a night when she had not been listening. Or perhaps her life's mate had smiled at her at one of the endless stream of parties, and she had been too preoccupied to see, and any meaningful dreams had been buried with her mother.

Then a classmate had shared plans of a year in Africa. She was going to work for Oxfam on their Fair Trade project, helping small farmers gain a greater share of the revenue from their products. The next day, Kayla had signed up for what she thought would be a sort of working vacation. Instead, she had found a passion worthy of investing her life.

Or so it had seemed, until the man she thought she knew had walked away with her project's funding. And broken her heart in the process.

Which had brought her home. To this. Sitting in her mother's chair, watching a stranger walk to the changing room and hand his new clothes back through the curtain.

She blinked away the sudden stinging and smiled as the salesman returned with a silver tea service. She cleared her throat and asked, "How do you take your tea?"

"I have no idea." Adam swept aside the red-velvet curtain and reemerged in a new shirt and slacks. "I don't have much experience with drinking tea in a shop."

"You'll find there's not much difference from drinking it anywhere else."

"Very funny." He sat on the seat next to hers, the tiny round table between them. Just as her mother and father had once sat. Kayla had loved to pour the tea, setting the silver strainer over the cup just as she did now . . .

"What's wrong, Kayla?"

Kayla felt the harmonies of planets in parallel orbit, just from Adam speaking those three quiet words. She knew tension had redrawn the angles of her face. She knew her chin had jutted in a fashion that made her look old. And her lips were tightly compressed. She had seen the expression often enough in her mirror over the past ten months.

Kayla needed both hands to steady the pot and pour the tea. "I was thinking of Africa."

Adam took the cup, let her add milk, declined sugar. "Tell me where you are."

Perhaps it was the way he spoke that last word. Where you *are*. Where her life is *now*. Not in the past. This very moment. She set down the pot, and said the first thing that came to her mind. "I drink a lot of tea in Africa. The water isn't safe unless it's boiled, and even boiled it still tastes horrid. So I drink tea all day long. All Westerners do. Tea or coke or bottled water, and sometimes the shipments of water from Europe don't come through. Our office has its own filtration system, and then we boil the water hard and use tea to mask the flavor."

She stared at the rear window and the tiny walled garden beyond. The intensity of Adam's gaze sent her soaring away, back to a world of yellow heat and eternal dust. She was there, and yet intensely here as well.

"Kayla."

She started. "Sorry. I was . . ."

"Away. Tell me what you are seeing."

"East Africa is in its third year of drought. The lack of rain dominates everything. All the trees around the cities have been chopped down for fuel. There is electricity a few hours each day, but the poorer families can't afford to use it, especially for cooking. The pennies they earn go for food. If there's any money left over, they send one child to school. Sometimes the eldest, sometimes the brightest. Whoever is lucky enough to shine. The others work. Everybody works all the time, and hopefully there's food to eat and money left over for the one lucky child to study."

She saw herself walking the yellow road from the compound where many of the Europeans lived to the project's offices. The compound was on the airport road, about a mile and a half closer to Dar es Salaam than the offices. She often walked the road in the cool of early dawn. If she missed her walk, it meant no exercise that day, because later the heat grew overpowering. The hour between night and day was very special. There was little car traffic, but the road was nonetheless very full. Children fortunate enough to go to school walked with their books and wooden tablets, for no family could afford the luxury of writing paper. The children who herded goats or the family cow watched the students with carefully blank faces, revealing neither envy nor the hopelessness of a life forever denied them. The dust was not so bad then, and the sky was awash in a gentle light. One of Kayla's tenets was that every family involved in her project had to place all their children in school. She was very strict about that. It meant she could walk the road and smile at the children, and feel that she was making a difference in other small lives.

She heard herself say, "The youngest children gather fuel. But as I said, there aren't any trees left. So they gather animal dung and thornbushes. And old bones. There are bones everywhere now. The fields are full of dust and animal carcasses picked clean. Fires of cow dung and thorn brush and dried bones give off an amazing aroma. I know it sounds horrid. But the smell is like some exotic spice. This morning I finally got round to unpacking my suitcases so I could give everything a proper wash. The smell took me straight back. It is in everything. Even my hairbrush."

Kayla stopped then. The words dried up entirely. For she had another image, one of Geoffrey entering the offices. He had always taken a taxi from the hotel where he had lived to the project. Geoffrey liked to say he wasn't above helping the unwashed masses, but he needed a proper start to the day. He was fastidious in his dress and almost foppish in his manners. But his smile and his charm and his incredible looks had been enough to mask the distance from which he had viewed life in Africa. Or so it had been, until that morning.

Kayla blinked and slowly came around. Adam watched her with an impossible patience. Impossible that a haircut and some new clothes could change him so much. His face looked leaner, his manner more polished. She felt a sudden desperate urge to claim he was just another thief, just another liar. Just like all men were bound to be.

Because to do otherwise would be to accept what her heart now whispered. That Adam was not merely different. Nor was he just a friend. The way he looked at her now invited Kayla to bridge the impossible divide and enter the forbidden zone. The zone beyond the walls that, up to now, she had called protection. The temptation hovered in the air between them, sparkling in the sunlight upon gossamer wings of invitation.

She whispered, "We really should be going."

chapter 9

$\mathcal{T}$hey took a taxi back to Adam's residence, his purchases piled on the seat between them. He hurried up to his room, dropped off the gear he was not now wearing, then returned to the street fearing she would use the interruption as an excuse to change the subject. When he settled into the old Mercedes, he asked, "Who was the guy who broke your heart?"

Kayla started the car. "His name was Geoffrey Rambling."

"A name like that, he had to be British."

"Extremely. We met in Nairobi. I was down for a conference. He claimed to have been a consultant to the ministry of finance, sent there by his UK bank." She put the car into gear. "Daddy's board insisted that I hire a qualified business manager."

"They financed your project?"

"Oxford Ventures hoped to use my work as a centerpiece for a new ad campaign. Daddy has always been big on giving back to the community. The way he put it to the board was, 'We now operate in a *global* village.'"

"Very smart."

"Not smart enough to keep their money safe."

"So you hired Geoffrey and he stole from the project. How much?"

Their rumbling passage down the gravel drive nearly masked her words. "Over six hundred thousand pounds."

As they climbed the company's front stairs, Adam asked, "How long do you have? Before you go back, I mean."

Kayla heard the quick hesitation, and knew he had started to ask, *we*. How long do *we* have? "Daddy's birthday is next Friday. I'll stay for that."

Adam kept his face carefully impassive. "So, eight days."

"Yes."

"You can't stay for Christmas?"

As soon as the front doors opened, the receptionist said, "Ms. Austin, your father needs to see you immediately."

"Thank you." Kayla faced Adam. "I shouldn't stay even this long. But it would mean so much to Daddy."

"I see."

"Ms. Austin, your father was most insistent."

Kayla excused herself and walked to the chairman's suite. She entered her father's office in a wavering state. Her carefully constructed intentions that included no room for another man, the ones she had assumed were both binding and permanent, had new fault lines.

Her father was seated behind the desk, which was uncommon when there was a guest in his room. Peter Austin liked to treat all visitors as distinguished guests, employees included. Normally he led them to the sofa and saw to coffee, settling down only when they were comfortable. Yet now he sat ensconced behind his beechwood desk, his weary features creased into a frown. "She is here, Joshua. Ask her."

Joshua was seated across from him, his own anger very evident. "Give us your impressions of this Wright fellow."

Kayla walked to the chair normally reserved for Mrs. Drummond when there was a meeting that required minutes. But she did not sit down. Instead, she stood behind it and rested her hands on the back, as though placing a shield between her and the room. "He was very grateful that Daddy is giving him a chance."

"Not enough, I'm afraid." Joshua's gaze did not waver. "We seek insight into his character."

Kayla said, "Adam Wright is a real gentleman."

"Correction. He is an *actor*."

"Was," Peter said. "I believe you once did some amateur theatrics yourself."

Joshua flushed. "That was in college, as you well know. This man is a so-called professional, though the word scarcely fits the nonsense he portrayed."

"Do you mean to tell me you would have refused payment if someone had offered you a professional gig?"

Joshua crossed his arms. "I seek data. Your daughter has a singular ability to see to the heart of matters."

Not with Geoffrey Rambling, she silently corrected him. "Adam was completely uncomfortable with spending money, even though it was given to him specifically to kit him out."

Joshua erupted. "Really, Peter. You gave him money from the company accounts?"

Peter waved that aside. "So the man is miserly. Given what the company faces, I'd say it is a distinct advantage."

"Until we know more, I must insist that Wright not be permitted access to company matters."

"Don't be absurd, Joshua."

"Absurd, am I? What if he is another spy?"

"You have no evidence any such spy exists. Or even that MVP is after us."

"No, but I'm looking. It's only a matter of time before I ferret them out."

Peter sighed his exasperation and picked up the phone. "Mrs. Drummond, be so good as to ask Adam Wright to join us."

When he entered the chairman's office, Adam was greeted by a scene strong as a warning light. Peter Austin frowned mightily at something on his desk. Two chairs were drawn up to the desk's other side. Joshua Dobbins occupied one. Kayla stood behind the other, her fingers playing nervously on the back. She would not meet his gaze.

"You have him here, Joshua," Peter said. "Do get on with it."

The finance man said to Adam, "I want to know what proposals you intend to put forward."

"You gave me thirty days."

"Indeed you did, Joshua," Peter agreed. "You told me that yourself."

"If the man is half as good as you claim, he will not have arrived here empty-handed."

Adam confirmed, "Actually, I have been studying several possibilities since I met with Peter in Washington."

Peter's features cleared somewhat. "Have you indeed?"

"One is a German company. Herrstadt."

Joshua rose from his chair. "Spell that."

Adam did so. Joshua stepped in beside his chairman and typed into the computer. Joshua read off the screen, "Herrstadt's specialty is structural engineering. Traded on the Frankfurt exchange. Three hundred million euro turnover." Joshua glanced up. "Their stock is down forty-one percent for the year. Hardly a ringing endorsement."

Adam replied, "Herrstadt specializes in overseas public works projects. Bridges, roads, sewage systems. They won a major contract for rebuilding Basra, the main port city in Iraq. Four months ago, their two top engineers were kidnapped. Their men were freed, but the company has since pulled out of the country. They lost a ton in retainer, and they had no project to take up the slack. It's put them in the red for the year. They're listed on the Frankfurt exchange. Their stock tanked."

Joshua stood by the computer. He wore what was apparently his standard uniform of white shirt, dark pants, dark tie. His face was as starched and narrow as his clothes. "This is a reason to invest in them?"

"Before the civil crisis, they were the largest road builders in the Congo."

Joshua protested to the company chairman, "This is insane. The Congo makes the Iraq crisis look like a cakewalk."

"It did," Adam corrected. "But not anymore."

Peter said, "Let the man finish, Joshua."

"The United Nations has just pulled off the first free elections in forty years," Adam went on. "There is a growing sentiment among companies specializing in the developing world that the Congo is going to be the next big success story. The worldwide commodities market is exploding. Copper prices have doubled, silver is up five hundred percent. The Congo is a major supplier of both. The new government's first act was to sign a contract with Newland Mining for one new project with proven reserves of fifty million metric tons of copper ore, valued at four hundred billion dollars."

Joshua bent over the computer. "So we could invest in Newland. They're a sound company with solid footing in the Congo."

"Newland's stock is up sixty percent in the past three weeks."

Joshua typed, studied the screen, then glanced at Peter. The chairman said, "So we were late on Newland. Why this German firm?"

"To reopen the diamond mines and keep this new copper mine viable, there has to be stability. The UN has agreed to keep peacekeepers in the country for another four years. One of their stated aims is to supply protection directly to the builders of new infrastructure, especially roads to the outlying regions."

Joshua demanded, "How do you know Herrstadt is going to build them?"

"Because," Adam replied, "Herrstadt is the only company invited to bid."

Joshua said to the chairman, "How could he possibly know this unless they are granting him insider access?"

"Nobody has granted me anything," Adam retorted. "And who is 'they'?"

Peter asked in return, "Would you please explain to Joshua how you obtained this decidedly confidential information?"

"It was announced weeks ago. The financial press discounted it because of Herrstadt's pullout from Iraq. The chairman has since said their pullout was part of the ransom demand to free their two kidnapped executives."

"Or so you say."

"If you scroll down, you'll find it all in the company's latest quarterly update." Adam watched Joshua bend back over the keyboard, and added, "There's something else. Even facing this drastic loss and the slide in both stock price and earnings, they have not fired a single employee. Which strongly suggests they have a backup plan."

Peter asked, "How much do our foes have invested in companies relying on third-world projects?"

Joshua remained focused upon the computer screen.

"Nothing. Isn't that the correct sum, Joshua? Nothing whatsoever?"

Adam asked again, "Who do you think I'm spying for?"

Peter said, "Would the both of you be so good as to give us a moment alone?"

Adam followed Kayla from her father's office. He did not need an analyst's brain to see the facts branded in the air before his eyes. The company was in dire peril, and even if it managed to survive a bit longer, Joshua Dobbins wanted him gone. Kayla was leaving, her own dreams in tatters. His pocket was full of money he had not earned, he was dressed in clothes for a job he might not have tomorrow, and his heart was wrenched by the thought of losing a woman he had known for one day. "Let's go for a walk."

He did not speak again until they were outside the front doors and Kayla was shivering in a wind he could not be bothered to feel. Adam took off his jacket and draped it around her shoulders. "I know you've got a world full of reasons not to trust me, and if you refuse I won't try again. But like I told you in town, I want to help. And the only way I can do that is if you tell me what's going on."

To her credit, Kayla neither hesitated nor asked what he was talking about. "Before he started this company, Daddy worked for a company called Madden and Van Pater—"

"Sure. They're known as MVP." Adam made no attempt to hide how impressed he was. "You see their ads everywhere. MVP, the most valuable player on your financial team."

Kayla went on, "When Daddy left, he took some of their clients. They've been gunning for him ever since. Daddy is convinced they're behind this latest crisis." She swept the hair out of her face. "He was arguing with Joshua this morning, saying they needed to hire a detective to see if they could find any evidence to back his assumptions. Joshua insisted it was too dangerous, that MVP has a spy in place and would love nothing more than to use news of an investigation to fire up a public scandal."

"We could hire an independent detective agency. See what we can dig up."

"With what?"

"The money you gave me."

The air slipped from her in a long sigh.

"I don't care what you say, Kayla. I haven't earned it and I don't like the idea of taking a handout." Another thought hit him. "While we're at it, we might as well hunt for your thief."

"What?"

"You said he was a banker, right? What was his name?"

"Geoffrey Rambling."

"Right. Was his bank British?"

"I already thought of that. The bank has never heard of him. It was just another lie. One of a billion."

"This bank where he supposedly worked, where does it operate?"

"In the City. The financial district of London."

"They say the most successful lies are those that parallel the truth. So we ask the same PI to see if Rambling worked somewhere near that bank. Do you have a photograph?"

"I burned them all."

"And the name he gave you is probably bogus." He read her expression as serious incredulity. "Well, maybe it wasn't such a good idea after all."

Kayla reached one hand up and around the back of his neck. Pulled him down. And kissed him on the cheek. Soft, almost sisterly, a fragile touch, there and gone in an instant.

But a kiss just the same.

Adam breathed an astonished, "Wow."

"That was a mistake."

"Not from where I'm standing."

"You don't know me, you have no ties to us or our problems, and here you are, doing your best to help."

"It's not much." His heart was racing now, trying to deal with the aftershock. "Kayla, let me invest the money your father gave you for your project."

She headed back inside. "I need to talk this over with Daddy."

"Don't take too long. Every day counts in this business."

"Believe me, Adam, I know that all too well."

chapter 10

That evening, Professor Beachley's entire household came out to see them off. Two of the lodgers, both older than Adam, complained that the professor should have asked them if she had wanted to go.

"I did not ask Adam," she replied, using her walker to make it down the front lane. "I merely accepted his invitation."

Mrs. Brandt placed the wheelchair in the taxi's trunk, then watched approvingly as Adam helped the old lady settle into the rear seat. She took the walker from Adam and said, "She's right, you know. You were a dear to ask her."

The town center was packed with students rushing to services. Their robes flapped behind them like broken wings. When they pulled up in front of Christ Church, Adam paid the taxi and settled her into the wheelchair. He maneuvered the chair beneath the towering college gates, doing his best to keep the chair steady as it jounced over uneven flagstones. As they passed through the broad college portal, a man in a dark suit and odd bowler hat emerged from the porter's lodge, his weathered face creased in smiles. "Professor Beachley, as I live and breathe."

"So nice to see you again, Lester. How is the wife?"

"Growing old before her years, Professor. Wishing she could serve up this latest crop of students in a stew."

"No doubt the two of you will have them trained in time." She reached back to pat Adam's hand upon the handle. "This is one of my lodgers, Adam Wright."

The porter touched one chapped hand to the rim of his hat. "Sir."

"Adam works for Peter Austin's firm. You remember his late wife, Amanda."

"Like it was yesterday. Many was the time I chased her daughter off the main fountain."

"Do give your wife my best. Come along, Adam. We mustn't be late."

The main quadrangle was impossibly large, ringed in ancient stone buildings as ornate as a square crown. The early December dusk transformed the central fountain into a play of water and shadows. The wheelchair squeaked softly as they entered a quieter realm, one entirely removed from the city beyond the gates. Dr. Beachley sighed, "Isn't it wonderful?"

"Amazing."

"I do so miss the old place." She pointed to her right. "The far door was once my family's abode. Isaac Newton lived there in another time."

He glanced over, but saw nothing save shadows. Overhead, the stars were being erased by a sweep of coming rain.

"Henry the Eighth was one of the college's main benefactors." Her casual tone made it sound like the donation had arrived the previous week. "The colleges who protested Henry's formation of the Anglican Church treated us like lepers. But Christ Church has always made a habit of going against the grain."

From the outside, the church was just another door set in the quad's far corner. Inside, however, a different realm was revealed. Adam waited patiently while one robed figure after another greeted Dr. Beachley. She was careful to introduce him, but Adam paid little attention to the stream of people, save for the smiles that wreathed all their faces. Dr. Beachley entered the main chapel surrounded by a bevy of professors who insisted upon settling her wheelchair by the dons' high-backed benches and then made a space for Adam.

All save Dr. Beachley rose for the choir to enter, who were led by crimson-robed clergy. The only illumination came from soft lights upon the stained-glass windows and candles in tall crystal globes. Hundreds and hundreds of candles. When they were again seated, Dr. Beachley motioned him closer. "Most of this church hails from the fifteenth century. But the floor and pillars and some of the stained glass date from the original cathedral of Oxford, one of the first erected in England, so old the dates mingle with the dust." She pointed at the huge round stained-glass window opposite them, of a knight in armor slaying a dragon. "Legend has it the glass was made while Saint George was still alive. Which between you and me is a bit of old rubbish."

The all-male choir sang John Tavener's rendition of "The Lamb," the voices young and crisp and vibrant. The priest then rose and gave the packed hall a formal blessing. Dr. Beachley sighed in pure pleasure and patted his hand. "You have made an old lady very happy."

The stone hall was built to the proportions of a different era, so tall the carved roof swam in the candlelight. The pillars were broad as redwoods. The floor flowed and rippled with the currents of time. The hall was built as a long and narrow cross, with the pews set to face one another across the central aisle. The pews rose in stairlike order, the nave at the front and the choir at the far end by the doors. The nave was separated from the main hall by a thousand-year-old screen. The stained-glass windows were five stories tall. The audience rustled as they sat once more. The service continued in a cadence from a time beyond time. The choir and the priest both alternated between Latin and English. The seats, the screen, the altar, the speaker's platform, the roof, were all stained by centuries of candle smoke. The Bible was big as a gilded sail and rested upon a stone eagle whose claws held a golden crown.

The rain arrived while the priest spoke. It fell and fell, a gentle river of the night. The priest ended his homily and the choir sang, "Oh hush the noise, ye men of strife, and hear the angels sing!"

Adam could not escape the rush of memories that flowed with the rain. The reminiscences fell in a constant cadence, the images passing in a wash of helpless regret. His father had vanished when he was four, just walked out one day and never returned. His mother had never lost her smile in front of Adam, but at night he could hear her weeping through the walls of their dismal apartment. Adam listened to his mother's anguish and swore in a little boy's manner that no one would ever hurt him like that. Never.

His mother had fled into the arms of her church. Every hour she did not spend with her son or working was given to church activities. And she worked all the time. She photographed babies for two local department stores, she photographed weddings, she shot photos for school yearbooks. She was quick and professional and never lost her smile, not even when facing a thousand sullen teenagers in a week that never seemed to end. Adam remembered how she hated doing school photos most of all, being reduced to an automaton on the other side of a camera. Yet even then she did not complain so much as state in her matter-of-fact way that she would be glad when the week was over. The week, the month, the year after year of a life that had been foisted upon her by a man who left and a son who loathed her church as a place for losers. That was how Adam described it, after running away from Sunday school at age twelve. A place he hated, because they wanted to teach him to forgive. And he would never forgive his father. Not in a hundred billion years.

His mother had been forced to give up her dream of becoming a freelance photographer, the next Eve Arnold, so that she could support them. She did what she had to in order to give them a steady income, even shooting high school students with their nose rings and tattoos and young hate. And when she came home, washed out and her eyes full of dead dreams, she would dredge up a smile for her son and say, "At least I've held on to what's most important in this small life."

And still the rain fell.

chapter 11

*O*ver dinner that night, Kayla related Adam's request to handle her investment funds. As she spoke, her father's gaze remained upon his wife. Honor listened as intently as Kayla's father.

Her father said, "You're going to trust Adam with your capital?"

"I'm thinking about it."

"That is remarkable," Honor said. "You have a thousand reasons not to trust any man ever again."

"There's something about Adam that reminds me of Geoffrey." Kayla related seeing the photograph at the receptionist's desk. "It's not who he is, it's what he once was. Arrogant. Aloof. Menacing even when he laughed."

"That's an actor for you," her father said, but he sounded uncertain.

Honor said, "I don't believe the man I met could ever have acted his way into such a role. Unless . . ."

Kayla studied the woman seated across from her father. In the distance, a single light glimmered deep in the night-shrouded valley. The fire in the living room crackled softly. The refrigerator hummed and then went silent. Kayla finished the thought in an almost whisper. "Unless something has changed him."

"Something immensely powerful," Honor agreed.

Kayla studied her father's wife. The unspoken question hung in the air between them; if that immense change had created a man she could trust.

"Adam also told me he wants to help the company."

"His investment suggestions were first-rate," Peter said.

"No. He wants to use the money you gave him and hire a detective to go after MVP."

Peter was rocked back in his seat. "The young man's offer makes Joshua's desire to fire him almost sadistic."

Honor asked, "What is Joshua after now?"

"He's canvassing the board as we speak. Looking for a majority that will back his plan to begin massive layoffs. And he'll start with Adam."

"I don't ever want him in this house again."

"Honor. Please."

"He's as desiccated as a museum artifact. He's bloodless. I would rather see—"

"Honor."

Kayla watched the exchange, saw how Peter's wife controlled herself with genuine effort. And liked her immensely as a result. Kayla said, "Adam knows he might be fired and still wants to do this. He thinks he could do it outside the firm and buffer the company, even if they do find out." She hesitated, then added, "He thinks I should use the same detective and try to locate Geoffrey."

"What a splendid idea," Honor said. "Track the louse down and demand your money."

"I wouldn't get my hopes up," Peter said. "You'd be accusing the man of a crime on a different continent, with no genuine liability or proof to hand."

"There's another problem. I burned all my photos of Geoffrey."

Honor said, "I have some. On my computer. You sent us several. I've kept them all." She smiled triumphantly. "And I still say it's a splendid idea."

That evening his mother phoned on his cell phone. Her news left him tossing and turning most of the night. She had called to tell him of yet another dream. One that resonated more strongly than any before.

The next morning, when the phone rang as he prepared for breakfast, Adam assumed it was his mother calling with yet another helping. Instead, Peter Austin said, "Look here, I'm sorry to bother you on a Saturday. But I thought, well, Kayla told us last night of your most remarkable proposal. I can't say which touched me more deeply, your offer to assist my daughter or your offer to assist my firm."

"I meant it," Adam said. "Every word."

"I personally am all in favor of giving both of your proposals a go. As for investing Kayla's funds, I assume she has told you about Geoffrey Rambling?"

"A bit."

"Our firm is at least partly to blame. We agreed to finance their expansion, but only if Kayla hired an experienced business manager. Of course, we had no idea his résumé would prove to be a bald fabrication, beginning with his name. At the time, Geoffrey Rambling seemed to be . . ."

"Ideal."

Peter's tone hardened with the iron frustration of a father wronged. "As financial officer, Geoffrey had cosignatory rights over the company accounts. Which granted him the access required to siphon off the money not yet invested."

"Which he did."

"Every cent. He was complete, I grant you that. He even went so far as to empty the office cash box." Peter hesitated, then said, "I suppose she told you that they were engaged to be married."

Adam rubbed the ribs over his heart. "Kayla skipped that bit."

Peter sighed. "Keep it between us, that's a good lad."

"When did all this go down? The theft."

"About ten months ago. Kayla kept it secret from even me until September. She was determined to make a go of it, although in much-reduced form. She almost did. Which, given the fact that she has no former business experience, and this is Africa we're talking about, is nothing short of astounding."

"So her trusting me with the project capital . . ."

"I take as a very good sign." Peter's tone became briskly professional. "Which brings us to your very kind offer to help us with this matter of hiring an outside investigator. Joshua has been adamant that our taking any steps to investigate the opposition would be more than futile, it would be dangerous. He is certain this group has spies inside our organization. They will know as soon as any such steps are taken. To go public with such news, especially if they have physical evidence, would be disastrous."

"The fact that you're only doing it to protect yourself from them—"

"Means less than nothing, since we ourselves have no hard proof." Peter hesitated, then went on, "I must warn you, young man. You may well not have a job after Monday."

"Kayla said as much."

"There is no further money coming from the company."

"I've gone without before."

"In that case, Kayla will be coming in to see you, and bringing some documents you might find of interest."

"Thanks for trusting me. That means a lot."

"If there is anything I can ever do to help you however small, you need only ask."

"That's not why I'm doing this."

"I understand. And that *is* why I make this offer."

Kayla left at mid-morning and drove the old Mercedes to Adam's boardinghouse. They took over the kitchen table and went to work, or at least Adam did. Kayla sort of drifted. Her night had been disturbed repeatedly by dreams of Geoffrey, and she'd woken up feeling drugged. Kayla gave Adam the name of an investigation agency her father had said came highly recommended. Adam used his new cell phone and spoke to the agent manning the office that Saturday morning. He ran through the proposed project with terse confidence. He then hooked Kayla's laptop to the kitchen phone and transferred the photos of Geoffrey Rambling that Honor had supplied. Adam then contacted the broker suggested by her father and arranged for the account to be set up and the investments to be made. Kayla watched as Adam went online a second time and transferred the funds from her bank to the new brokerage account. She stowed away the handwritten documents giving her the access codes without even looking at them.

Adam then led her into the front parlor, the one used by the students, and said, "Mom called last night. She's had another dream." He leaned his elbows on his knees and began describing what his mother had told him to the frayed carpet at his feet.

As she listened, Kayla felt an immense need to simply get *away*. She was on her feet before Adam even finished speaking. "How long do you need to get ready?"

He blinked with slow confusion. "What?"

"Your mother called last night because it was urgent, right? And you felt the same sense of resonance as before?"

"I guess so."

"Yes or no, Adam. This is too important for fiddling."

"Yes. All right. I felt it."

"So go pack your bag. I've got the car. We'll be gone over-night." She made sure he was fully focused on her, then asked, "I don't have to worry about you taking advantage of the situation, do I?"

"No," he replied. "You don't."

"So hurry."

"What about you?"

"We'll stop by the house on our way out of town. It's in that direction."

"You know where to go?"

"I think so. We'll see."

Adam rose and started for his room to pack his things. Then he turned back. She watched him taste that remarkable smile of his. "Thanks, Kayla. A lot."

She stood in the empty front parlor and stared at the dust motes dancing in the gloom.

Just friends.

She turned at the sound of gentle thumps proceeding across the front hall. The professor appeared in the doorway, leaning heavily upon her walker. "You are looking lovely this morning, Miss Austin. Have you come for tea?"

"No, actually, Adam and I . . ." She could not quite make out why she blushed at the words. "He needs help doing something for his mother."

"I gather she is unwell. Is it serious?"

"I'm afraid so."

"How sad. And how very good that he has you to offer aid in his hour of need." She was so bowed over the walker that she had to twist her neck in order to look at Kayla. "Are you two an item? Do they still say that these days?"

"I don't . . . No. No. We're not."

"Ah."

The space between them was suddenly a vacuum that drew out the words, "I have to return to my work. In Dar es Salaam."

"Love is such a dreadful impossibility. Such a treacherous task, to defy the world and offer one's heart." Her eyes sparked. "But Adam is so very fortunate nonetheless. To have a young woman who understands the trial and the loss he faces. It must mean the world to him."

"He's a good man."

"That he most certainly is. He made an old woman very happy last night." Dr. Beachley started to turn away, then added, "If you would permit me to offer one small bit of advice."

"Of course."

"I suspect he already has feelings for you. Oh, I am well aware that I hardly know either of you. But I suspect our young Adam cares more than he realizes."

"I can't see why."

"Can't you? How very curious. Do you see yourself as so very unappealing?"

"More like damaged goods."

"Yes, of course. The dire consequences of living in this jagged age. But you see, my dear, Adam is bound to you by that most remarkable bond. You know his pain. You understand what shapes his world. Whether you know it or not, whether *he* realizes it yet. He needs you." She made a slow process of turning back to the door. "Even if you feel you have none to give, you offer the young gentleman hope. Hope of a tomorrow beyond the looming maw of dank earth that awaits his mother. Hope of a future where he might stand where you are now. Making plans. Living your passions. Striving to patch over the fractures this life can make in one's most precious dreams."

Kayla would have protested that she had nothing of the sort to offer anyone, if only she could have found the breath. As it was, she was fortunate to find the chair before her legs gave way.

Adam found her seated on the horsehair sofa, staring blindly at the sunlight splashing upon the window. "Let's hit the road."

chapter 12

*A*dam drove because Kayla asked him to. The car was a magnificent beast of leather and chrome and polished burl and purring engine, with squared-off edges and thick sofa-style seats and less than twenty thousand miles on the clock. Even the turn signal ticked with stately calm. It was a vehicle made for Oxford, magnificent in a peculiarly dated way.

Driving on the opposite side of the road was far less difficult than Adam had feared. He simply followed the flow. They soon left the Ring Road and the Saturday shopping traffic behind. Kayla limited her conversation to a few terse directions. Adam could see something was bothering her. He feared it might have to do with her offer to accompany him on this new quest. But he felt no need to ask anything just then. Since his arrival in Oxford, his world had been filled with mystery and few solid answers.

The only thing he could say for certain was that he did not feel alone. Adam shared the morning's vulnerability with as strong a woman as he had ever known. He was thrilled by the prospect of spending the day in her company. He tried to remind himself that Kayla was leaving for Africa in just seven days. But driving this wonderful car down an increasingly empty road, headed toward a destination that made no sense whatsoever, left him wanting to shout out loud.

The sky had cleared after raining all night long. A strong wind blew across a crystal clear sky. The morning light bathed a distinctly English landscape, beautiful in a vacant wintry manner. Once they were into the rolling hills and quieter ways, Kayla said, "Tell me what your mother said."

"I did. Back in the front parlor. There isn't anything more."

"Tell me again."

"She saw me climbing the crest of a hill. The highest hill in the area. Round at the top. Partly covered by forest. There was a town down below, she counted three steeples. The bells were ringing. It was clear and cold. Behind me was a tower, like something from an ancient castle. I just stood there and looked over the valley and the town." He glanced over. And held his breath.

Kayla asked, "Your mother said climbing this hill was important?"

"The word she used was *vital*. It was vital that I go there."

"And you felt it was important too."

"I told you, Kayla. I thought it was the hospital calling. My heart was going about a thousand beats a minute. So it was hard to tell anything for certain. But yes. I guess I did."

"You're not telling me everything, are you?"

The wind drummed softly about the car. "Mom said I was happy."

Kayla did not speak.

"Not just happy. Content. Full of joy and wonder. Looking forward to a new and wonderful future." The words gummed up his mouth even after they had emerged. "Which is impossible."

Adam could not remember the last time he had faced a woman's parents. Not since high school, certainly. The two years he had spent acting professionally had cauterized all such memories, like passing from a schoolyard into a blast furnace.

He stood by the living room window and tried to come up with something proper to say. There was little privacy in the open-plan house. Which meant Adam heard the conversation between father, daughter, and stepmother taking place in the rear dining area. He could not hear the exact words, but he knew they were concerned. Yet the longer they talked, the more Adam wanted her to come. He had become very adept at wanting nothing and expecting less. But not today. So he scripted in his head what he would say to Peter Austin, how he did not intend anything improper, how they'd take separate rooms, how he respected the family, yada yada.

The conversation ended. Footsteps ran lightly up the stairs in the newer stone quarter. The upstairs floorboards creaked softly. Adam heard two voices approach. He found himself beset by first-date nerves.

Peter Austin held his wife's hand. He was dressed in Saturday gardening clothes. His features were creased with worry and fatigue, yet he still looked every inch the captain of industry. Craggy-faced, uncompromising gaze, deceptively mild voice. "Might I ask you something?"

"Sure."

"The way you identified the German company."

Honor said, "Peter, invite your guest to sit down. Offer him coffee."

"He'll be sitting for hours. They're going for a drive. Do you want coffee?"

"I'm good, thanks."

"There, you see? Niceties done. Back to my question."

"Herrstadt."

"Not the company. The process. How did you come by this?"

"You want to know how I structure my analysis."

"Precisely."

Adam knew the question was a test. He also knew it was out of line. Analysts lived by holding their cards close. Even so, he liked the question and the reason.

Either he trusted the man, or he didn't. The unspoken challenge went as follows: If you can't trust me with the secrets of your craft, why should I trust you with my daughter?

Adam heard the rapid tread of footsteps back down the stairs. Kayla popped into view carrying a minuscule shoulder bag, scanned their faces, and said, "You're grilling him."

"Very mildly," her father replied.

Adam told Peter, "I need to explain something."

"Daddy . . ."

Peter Austin replied, "This is important, Kayla." When his daughter dropped her bag and crossed her arms, he said, "Go on."

"There are a hundred thousand analysts out there following company numbers. Others make it their life's goal to be first in the know. And the largest group follow market trends. I don't have the resources to build a hunter-seeker team. And I can't stand graphs."

"So you fashioned for yourself a different course." Peter Austin nodded once. "I thought that about you the first time we chatted."

"I call it the macro process. I study historical fracture lines. Economic crises, war, raw material surges, major market cycles, political trends that affect markets."

"Any number of people search the past."

"Right. But there are two differences here. First I identify what I think is a trend in today's world. Then I go back and build historical data around past trends that follow as closely as possible what is happening *today*. I study companies that reaped the whirlwind. Who survived and prospered, and why. And the same for those that failed spectacularly. Then I look for parallels in today's market."

"History repeating itself," Peter Austin said.

Adam replied, "All the time."

"I like your response, young man," Peter Austin said. "I like it immensely."

Kayla said softly, "Can we go now?"

Kayla soon had them off the main road. She said the Cotswolds should only be visited on lanes less than ten feet wide. Adam drove because she asked. He felt happy for the first time since leaving America. No, it was longer than that. He scanned back, searching for a time when smiles had come easy.

"What's going on in that mind of yours?"

"Am I that easy to read?"

"Answer my question." But her tone was light.

"I was thinking about the day I put my mom on the plane to Africa. It was the first time I can remember actually giving her a lifetime dream." He shrugged. "Most of my life was spent being a major disappointment."

"You don't know that."

He did not answer, because to do so would mean giving in to the clouds, blocking out the sun that streamed straight through him.

"What was it like, acting in a television show?"

"Do you realize every time we've met, we talk about me and I hear almost nothing about you?"

"I don't like talking about myself."

"That makes two of us."

Kayla was quiet long enough for them to pass through a hamlet of stone and timber and wintry smoke. "So ask."

But he didn't. Not just then. Instead, he let the silence ease them through yet another tiny village. Kayla rode with a Cotswold Country map unfolded in her lap. There was no hint of civilization and modern times. The only road signs were wooden fingers planted alongside lanes that emerged from the stone walls and hedgerows. The narrow roads were burnished by a sunlight strong as heat. The landscapes were brown and earthy. Adam drove a grand old beast of a car, so broad he had to reverse away from incoming traffic, for the lanes were too narrow to permit anyone to pass them except where he could ease into a farm lane or lay-by. He kept his speed to thirty miles an hour. He did not care how long it took to get wherever they were going. Or if, in fact, they ever arrived at all.

Finally Kayla did as he had hoped. She sighed, and for once the sound was not full of the tension that etched her features and carved shadows in her cheeks. Instead, it was a sound of release. Kayla eased down to where her head rested on the seatback. Her hair spilled over the leather, russet upon brown.

Adam wanted to hear her voice without the stress, without the worry. But all he could think to say was, "This is one amazing car."

Then he was glad, because Kayla smiled. It was a rare gem of an expression, for it softened her. He slowed further, so he could look over and drink in the sight of this very different lady.

Kayla said, "It was my mother's. Daddy kept it mostly for the memories. He hates to drive."

He waited to see if she would talk about her mother. Or explain why her father preferred not to sit behind the wheel of such a machine. But Kayla remained as she was, watching the lane ahead, in silence. And Adam decided not to ask anything more just then, content with the easy silence and the day.

They bought cheese, stone-ground bread, and apples from a village shop. They ate at a stream with a rock as both table and bench. The valley was steep-sided, shielding them from the wind. Sheep supplied the entertainment, calling in cadence to the rushing water.

Adam decided it was time to ask, "Would you tell me about your project?"

Kayla stared at the water. "It all seems a million miles away right now."

"Forget the bad stuff. Practically all I've heard so far has been about the guy and the damage. Tell me the good."

She looked at him. The sun played upon her gaze, turning it to russet gemstone, clear as the stream that rushed beside them. "There was a lot of it. The good. A lot."

It seemed the most natural thing in the world to do as she had done in the coffee shop. Adam reached over and took hold of her gloved hand.

Kayla stared at the two hands, one bared and the other in leather. Adam waited for her to break the moment and say they needed to be getting on. But when Kayla lifted her hand free, it was merely to slip the glove off. She settled her fingers back into his and said, "How much do you know about Oxfam?"

"The name only."

"In the middle of the Second World War, the college chapels got together with the city churches and founded the Oxford Famine Relief Committee. Their aim was to bring food and shelter to the innocents of Greece and Netherlands who had been made homeless by the war. Other British cities set up similar groups, but Oxfam was the only one that kept going after the war. Oxfam now operates in seventy-four countries. They are often the first to bring supplies to disaster-hit regions and the last to leave. Their aim is not merely to feed and shelter the destitute, but once the crisis is under control, to help rebuild shattered lives.

"Before the drought struck East Africa, Oxfam helped start a worldwide project called the Fair Trade Initiative. In many of the poorest countries, farmers who raise the crops receive almost none of the profits. They are told what to grow by middlemen, who then pay them in seed and supplies, creating modern servitude. Oxfam sought to break this stranglehold by taking the place of the middlemen and giving all the profits back to the farmers and their villages."

The sun touched the lip of the western slopes. Instantly the sky overhead was filled with an orchestral array. Every tree, every rocky outcropping, became a symphony of light and tone. Adam drank in the day and the brook and the countryside perfumes, knowing Kayla was no longer entirely there beside him. She had drifted away, captured by a hot and dusty realm.

"No one expected the level of success Oxfam experienced with this project. Nowadays, many of Europe's supermarket chains have entire aisles for Fair Trade products. The result has been an anchoring of entire regions. Villagers were no longer giving up on land their families had farmed for generations and migrating to the cities. Why should they, when they could remain where they were and earn a decent wage and send their children to school and preserve their way of life." Kayla was silent for a moment before adding, "Then disaster struck."

Adam guessed, "The drought."

"Oxfam is now the major supplier of food and shelter to nine hundred thousand people in East Africa. The problem is, more than *four million* people are starving. Oxfam's central committees in Kenya and Tanzania and Ethiopia and Eritrea had to make a critical choice—continue to support the Fair Trade projects or feed the starving. They really had no option, not when faced with the prospect of babies dying if they didn't change directions."

Shadows drifted east until twilight's gentle blanket slipped over their resting place. The temperature dropped with the sun. Adam saw his breath as he said, "So they gave the project to you. Smart."

"They had just started to organize the farmers of northern Tanzania and southern Kenya when the drought hit. The areas where water remained plentiful were growing flowers that required enormous amounts of handwork. Asparagus, artichokes, some fruit trees. But the biggest crop by far was coffee. We continued where Oxfam had been forced to stop, building drying sheds, setting up a sorting operation and cold-storage facility for cut flowers and out-of-season vegetables."

Adam massaged the fingers going cold in the frigid dusk. "How many people were you helping, Kayla?"

She was quiet for a time, then used the hand that was still gloved to swipe at the edges of her eyes. "Almost a hundred villages. I wish you could have seen it when we were going strong." Her voice was not broken, not really. Just trembling hard, as though revealing the joy was only possible if she shared the sorrow as well. "We would go into the villages to deliver their quarterly paychecks. They would line the road. If you can call a dusty track through the veld a road. They sang us in, they sang us out. This region, the north of Tanzania and the south of Kenya, is mostly Kikuyu and very strong Christian. They gave us names. They called me . . ."

Adam reached over and enfolded her in his arms. She did not actually cry. Adam understood. She was strong, and the sorrow was old. She just needed a moment to collect herself. Oh, yes. He understood all too well. When she started to straighten, Adam released her, knowing she needed to rely on her own strength. After all, she was going back. She had to fight this battle to the bitter end. Alone. She was going in seven days.

The internal reverberation increased to the point that his voice was almost as unsteady as hers. "We need to be going."

$\mathcal{T}$he road crested a rise so high Adam caught a final teardrop of sunset gold amid the crown of trees. They descended with a tumbling river for company. A valley opened, wide enough to welcome both them and the river. Steep-sided hills brooded on all sides, bearing their cloaks of night like sentinels from an age of armor and warlocks, of seers and white-bearded kings. The sun was gone from this realm, yet the sky maintained its abundance of dusky hues. At the vale's heart rose a village of stone that glowed in the final light. The dominion of Broadway began with a sign declaring its royal charter of 1134. The central road deserved the village's name, for it was wide as a four-lane highway, yet paved in stone as ancient as the houses. At the village's heart was a coaching inn, with a domed entrance where carriages drawn by six matched steeds had once passed. Planted at the roadside was a sign declaring in Gothic script that the inn was the oldest in all England.

Kayla spoke for the first time since leaving their rocky haven. "Let's stay here."

Kayla had not taken so much time dressing for a dinner in a long time.

Her bathroom was almost as large as her bedroom. A huge tub stood on four lion's paws beneath a window she soon frosted with steam. She used all the hotel's wide array of free gifts—herbal shampoo and bath salts and conditioner and lotion, all from the same shop that supplied Buckingham Palace. She dried her hair, combed it carefully, and held it away from her face with her mother's jeweled clip. Kayla had decided not to take the jewelry pieces she had inherited from her mother to Africa, which was the only reason she still had them in her possession. Her watch, a graduation present from her father, and the one necklace she had in Dar es Salaam were gone now. In the weeks after Geoffrey vanished, Kayla had found these small thefts the hardest to bear. It felt as though he had stolen them intentionally to rub her nose in the dust. To break her just as hard as he possibly could.

And now there was Adam.

She sat in her slip before the little makeup table and oval mirror. The table was an old-fashioned affair, with a padded top and pink lace draped around the edges and a matching padded stool. The mercury-backed mirror rested in a gilded frame, with two miniature chandeliers dangling to either side. In the mirror Kayla could see a four-poster bed so high the hotel supplied an embroidered footstool to climb in and out. Across from the bed hung a portrait of a young woman, her face almost lost to candle soot.

She knew she would remember every little item about this room and this day for a very long time.

She lined up her makeup items like little chess pieces. She had not used any of them in months. The powder compact was cracked as the parched earth of Africa. The lipstick was almost gummy. The eyelash brush was rock-hard and left her dabbing gobs instead of evenly applying the ink. But she was able to achieve the un-made-up look she preferred. She finished with a trace of perfume behind each ear. She screwed the top back on the tiny bottle. One by one she placed the containers back in the little pouch. Then she lifted her gaze.

And stared straight into the truth.

Her father was right. Adam was a good man. He deserved far better and far more than the few fractured minutes she had to give.

Kayla rose from the stool. She picked up the dress on the bed. It was a midnight blue Feraud, high-collared and long-sleeved, fashioned of merino wool so fine it floated cloudlike over her head and clung invitingly to her form. She slipped into stockings and shoes to match. She drew out her mother's pearls from her shoulder bag's side pocket, and stepped back to the oval mirror.

Kayla fumbled with the clasp, then dropped her hands and said to her reflection, "You were a fool to come."

Even in the off-season, the two single rooms cost more than Adam paid for a month at the Oxford boardinghouse. He mused over how little this bothered him as he showered. He had never spent money easily. In his youth, there had been none to spend. When older and earning, he had always been too focused on the goal of future freedom. Adam dressed in the suit he had purchased with company money. He had felt silly packing a suit and dress shirt and new tie. Yet now, as he took the carved wooden staircase down to the main gallery, he was doubly glad, both because all the men he saw were equally well dressed, and because Kayla would no doubt have come prepared.

The hotel's main gallery was an odd juxtaposition of the antiquated and the polished. The flagstone floor still had grooves where metal-wheeled carts had brought in the packing chests used by guests arriving for the season. The front door was peaked and banded in iron, and each time one of the liveried servants opened it, Adam spotted another car from his dreams—a Bentley sports car, an Aston Martin, a vintage Rolls. The fireplace burned logs four feet long, casting a glow over the easy smiles and the dripping jewels. A giant Christmas tree draped in baubles and lights added to the festive atmosphere.

Then the glittering guests all turned in unison, the quick jerking motions of people whose attention has been drawn by the unexpected. And he knew. Even before he turned, he knew.

Kayla descended the staircase with careless ease. She wore a simple frock of understated elegance. It flowed about her, revealing both her feminine form and her strength. A string of pearls glowed softly in the firelight. A hairpin shaped like a tiny ruby butterfly looked ready to take flight. But it was not merely her beauty that captivated the guests. Kayla's presence was like a panther among caged and sheltered pets. Her tanned features were almost feral in the firelight. A distilled quality of strength and hard-earned wisdom emanated from her, stronger and far more alluring than perfume.

Adam watched her cross the gallery toward him and knew he was lost.

Dinner was served in the baronial hall. The maître d' bowed them through the double doors and led them beneath a ceiling forty feet high. All the tables cast glances their way. Every one.

When they were seated and the leather-bound menus were on the table before them, Adam said, "You're like some incredibly exotic bird that's just happened to land in the midst of all these English sparrows."

"Sometimes I feel so utterly foreign here. I don't know if it's the result of my mother insisting I be educated in America, or if I was just born without the ability to fit in anywhere."

"I know just exactly what you mean."

"In America I was too English. In Africa I had to prove to every native that I wasn't another overbearing Westerner, driven to travel by my own selfish agenda. And here I am *baffled* by these people. I watch the English, and it seems like they dance to music I never hear." She began rearranging her cutlery. "And they *lie* so well, with such polish and oily courtesy."

Adam reached across and took her hand. "He's not here, Kayla. Not tonight."

She stared at his hand. "I feel a little undone right now."

"I'm glad you still feel comfortable enough to tell me that."

"Perhaps too comfortable."

"There's no such thing."

"This afternoon leaves me feeling like I've opened a door and I can't get it shut again. No matter how much . . ." She looked at him with naked appeal. "So no more questions tonight, okay? Don't ask me anything. Just for a little while."

"Whatever you want. Tonight it's your turn. Ask away."

"You say that too easily. You make it seem so . . ."

He loved finishing that thought. "Natural?"

The waiters all wore white dinner jackets and seemed to skate beneath the tall ribbed ceiling. Kayla ordered wild salmon on saffron rice, he the Welsh lamb. Upon the walls brooded portraits of ermine-robed nobles. The paintings were flanked by royal standards. They were seated opposite a fireplace large enough to swallow their table. The room was scented by crackling cedar logs. Tall leaded windows rose by their table. The night-stained glass reflected a wash of candles.

He turned from the window to find Kayla watching him. He said, "Back in the valley where we stopped for lunch. You know how the sky looked after the sun disappeared behind the ridge? Photographers call that blue light, after the sun is gone but while the illumination is still strong enough to shoot without flash."

"Your mother taught you that?"

"It was her favorite time of day. A pro knows to tighten the aperture right down. That's where amateurs make their big mistake, opening the eye up broad so they can hand-hold the camera. But blue light is subtle. The camera has to be coaxed to capture the hues. Tighten the aperture, use a tripod, hold the exposure for as long as it takes. The colors become strong and gentle at the same time. She told me all this after her trip to Africa."

He stopped because the waiters arrived with their meal. They murmured pleasure over the food, traded bites from one another's plates. Like normal people. Finally Kayla said, "Finish that thought about Africa."

"Mom's group landed in Dar es Salaam at dawn. She spent the day walking. When the day went blue, she shot a photo that almost mirrors the one on your father's wall. You can't imagine the shock I felt walking in and seeing it hanging there."

"Actually, I can. The first year or so, I regularly e-mailed Daddy pictures. For the past nine months, I scarcely wrote at all. Then I walked into Daddy's office and there they were. And over dinner that night I learned Honor was the reason they were there." Kayla examined him intently. "How is it possible to talk with you like this?"

"I don't know, Kayla. But I feel the same way."

"I *never* discuss myself."

"Two pros at keeping secrets, talking easy as daylight." He lifted his hands. "It's a mystery. But I like it."

"Do you?"

"So much it scares me."

But it was Kayla who shivered.

"So ask away, Kayla."

"You're sure?"

"Let's see where it takes us."

She took a breath. "Why don't you ever mention your father?"

"He disappeared when I was four."

"Oh, Adam."

"Just walked out and never came home. My mother was working freelance for a couple of local newspapers and trying to build a portfolio. When my father left, all that was ditched. She switched to department stores shooting babies."

"And lived her dreams through the Eve Arnold prints."

"Mom covered the walls of our apartment with shots from a woman who had started out just as low and unknown."

"But she got the break your mother never had. I'm so sorry."

Adam was two people. The guy who spoke, and a guy who watched. Splintered by the impossibility of talking about things he never mentioned. And more than that. *Wanting* to speak.

And Kayla. This striking woman of force and shadow, a lady who feared his questions, was drawn so tightly she pushed aside the plates so she could reach across the table and take hold of both his hands. Pulling them together and enveloping them with her own. Adam looked at the strong tanned fingers gripping his. As though she had been doing it for years.

Natural.

Kayla said very softly, "Are you very close to her?"

"Not for a long time. But now. Yes. Very close."

"What happened before?"

"When I was little, Mom made me promise I wouldn't hate my father. She made it like the most important thing in her world, if I'd do this one thing. So I tried. For her."

The intimacy was strong as the heat radiating off the fire. "But it didn't erase the hate, did it?"

He shook his head. "No."

"So you rebelled."

"Not like you'd expect. Not the drugs or the tats or hanging with the losers. I just became a professional loner. My one goal in life was to never let anybody ever hurt me like my dad hurt my mom."

"And you," Kayla whispered. "He hurt you too."

Unseen hands swept the plates off the linen tablecloth. The waiter disappeared. Adam replied, "And me."

"You became an analyst."

"It's the perfect role for a loner. Lock myself in a room, study and fight against the world. Take all my money and gamble it on being the first. The smartest. The best."

"And the acting," Kayla said, walking right alongside him. "Letting you be other people. And getting paid for it."

"That was such a trip." He smiled at their collection of hands. "The television company came to my university acting class, saying they were looking for a local stud. That's exactly how they put it. A young heartbreaker who liked the lights."

Adam stared at his reflection in the window, his features flickering and flowing in the frosted glass. The night was filled with the immense prospect of becoming a different man.

Kayla tossed and turned all night. Adam's voice echoed through her darkened bedroom.

The drive had been bad enough. His presence had graced the bare winter landscape with an electric quality. But the dinner had almost done her in. Adam had not merely confessed. He had sent invisible magnets across the table that attached to her. Tore her through the carefully prepared barriers. Ripped open all the permanently sealed doors. Made her want to *believe* again.

She rolled over and turned on the bedside lamp. The light was a feeble wash that scarcely reached the room's far corners. The ceiling above her four-poster bed was oak planks with massive crossbeams. In a happier moment, she might have imagined herself nestled within a ship of the night. Being carried off to some distant shore, where hope was not a painful barb, where the good life was hers to claim.

The painting on the wall opposite her bed caught her eye. It was just another portrait. The hotel contained hundreds. This one was of a maiden in an era of starched crinoline caps and languid smiles. Candles and torches and time had darkened the woman's complexion and smoked away her clothes. In the lone bedside light, all Kayla could see clearly was the hand resting on her chin, a corner of her chair, and her face. Four spots of color in a broad canvas of black and gray. They held her, these glimpses of light in a sea of dark. A touch of hope that defied the surrounding night.

Kayla fumbled for the light switch and cast the bedroom back into darkness. But the woman's smile would not be vanquished so easily. It floated in the night, just beyond the bed, smiling at her. *Inviting* her.

Kayla flipped the covers over her face. Adam's smile floated before her eyes. Once again he held her hand upon the tablecloth, and once more her fingers hummed with the evening's still-perceptible power. She hungered for a night without fear and a tomorrow lived in hope. She didn't ask for gaiety or unending joy or a realm where all her dreams might come true. All she wanted was the simple gift of a good day. That and the touch of a man who reached for her in love.

chapter 14

They left Broadway the next morning. Adam drove through a monochrome day. Clouds loomed to the south, bunching tightly around the cliffs, poised to spill over and drench the valley. The sun had not yet crested the eastern ridge. The sky overhead was veiled with clouds not yet dense enough to blot out the day. Here and there Adam saw faint patches of blue. The river was the color of slate.

At Kayla's direction, Adam took a small lane that meandered behind the village church and then began the ascent. Adam drove to a plateau and pulled into a small parking lot. He leaned over the wheel and stared up at a very steep hill.

Kayla asked, "Is that it?"

"Maybe. I won't know until I reach the top."

She looked so small, seated there beside him. Her normal force had shrunk to where she seemed scarcely able to claim the space her body required. Kayla said, "I hope you find what you're seeking."

The hill stood like a lonesome old man, isolated from its neighbors by a river. Adam crossed a stone bridge stained with lichen. The water murmured with the wind and the chattering branches. The hill stood solemn in its mantle of wintry brown. Adam hiked across a bowl-shaped pasture and began up the rise. Part of him kept repeating words in time to his tread, *It's only a hill.* He would climb to the top and have a look around and return down and they would drive away.

But his mother's softly spoken challenge buffeted him far harder than the wind. She had said he would be happy at the top of this hill, a grand future ahead of him.

He had the wintry path all to himself. The few remaining leaves rustled impatiently as he passed. The wind made a gentle thunder in his ears. The higher he climbed, the more the sky became covered with a dense gray froth.

He crested the rise and faced a tower gray as the wintry day. The structure was medieval in design, a lone watchtower, so old in appearance it might have heralded from the realm of myth and fable. A crown of stone teeth ringed the top. Adam stood and wished for the tower's ability to ignore storm and winter and solitude.

He knew precisely why his mother's dreams disturbed him so. They rocked his world. Not merely with the resonance they carried inside himself. With their *challenge.* Her gentle words always contained something that urged him to move outside the walls he had erected around his life.

The wind buffeted him as he turned slowly. He was encircled by other hills, barriers of stone and earth that mocked his own internal fortress.

To his left, a cluster of wildflowers had grown inside a crevice. The surrounding rocks had protected the blossoms from the season. The thistle had dried to perfection, awaiting his hand. He plucked four pastel goblets of lavender and turquoise and placed them under his sweater for protection. He took another long look around as a crow called a solitary salute. He stared down at where the Mercedes waited, the only car in the lot. He felt his chest rise and fall. He felt his fingers go numb. He felt the wind reach through his sweater and chill the sweat on his chest.

The words rose unbidden inside his heart and mind, a gentle whisper that drowned out the wind. If only he knew how to love her.

They held to a communal silence until Adam was back inside the Oxford Ring Road and heading through Summertown toward his boardinghouse. He said, "I'm sorry I've been so quiet."

"You don't need to apologize. Not for that. Ever."

"I owe you an explanation. It's just . . ."

"Adam." She waited until he stopped at a light and could look over to continue. "You made the trip. You climbed the hill. But you didn't find what your mother said you would. It's only natural that you feel deflated."

Behind them, a car honked. Adam turned his attention back to the rain-swept road. "It's more than that. I feel like I let Mom down."

He drove slowly and listened to the ticking clock and the

tires slice through the wet. Adam expected her to come back with something about how he had done exactly as his mother had asked. How none of this was his fault. On the level of logic, he knew all this was true. Even so, he felt far more unsettled than when they had started off. Partly from what he had failed to find on the knob. But more because of what he had. He made the turn into Norham Gardens. The lane was quiet and empty beneath dark winter trees. Adam parked the car and glanced at the woman seated beside him. Six days.

Kayla said, "I have a problem. It's about Honor."

"Your father's wife."

Kayla avoided his gaze by fastening her attention upon the thistles he had brought down from the mountaintop. They were tied with her hair ribbon and set upon the dash. "This trip home is the first time I've seen Honor in over a year. The last time I came back was to tell Daddy that Geoffrey and I were getting engaged. I arrived to learn he was thinking about getting married again."

"You didn't come back again for your own father's wedding?" When she did not respond, Adam said, "That's pretty cold, Kayla."

"Daddy married for the second time four years after Mom died. I'll never forget the way he told me about her. Nothing about who this woman was or how great she was. Only that he was lonely. I called her Mrs. Two. I know, it sounds horrid, but I was sixteen and angry that my father was being disloyal to my mother's memory. That's how it felt. And Mrs. Two was a nightmare. She was addicted to labels. She had the most wretched laugh. Like an old-fashioned cash register, you know how the keys clanged? That was her laugh. If she had any heart at all, it was measured in carats and hidden in the back of her jewelry safe. Ten months after they married, I used university in America as my excuse to flee. She lasted another year, then filed for divorce. She made all sorts of horrid claims, going for Daddy's jugular. The only thing that saved Daddy was that Joshua had detectives tracking Mrs. Two for months. They discovered some fairly awful things."

"Good old Joshua."

Kayla was silent for a time, then turned and looked at him. "It's so easy to break rules with you."

"Go on with your story."

"Honor was impossibly young and beautiful. And Daddy was so happy."

"You thought he was going down for round three. You felt you had to warn him. This is natural, Kayla."

"It wasn't like that. Well, maybe a little. I came home to talk about *my* love."

Adam dropped his gaze to the hand held by both of his. "Your love."

"Yes."

"Geoffrey."

"He said he was so fascinated with me and my project that he would toss aside his consultancy contract and take the managerial position without salary. He *said* . . ."

Her voice trailed off. Adam listened to rain spatter the car's roof. "What does this have to do with Honor?"

"She warned me. Or tried to. She asked me questions that *hurt*." Kayla's words came in a sudden rush. "Was I right to trust him so fully after just coming to know him. Was he genuinely able to satisfy my lifetime longings. Was he a man who revealed his motives as well as his desires. I'd come home to tell Daddy how happy I was. Instead, I discovered him with a woman he had not been able to write me about, since he knew how much I loathed Mrs. Two, and he wanted this one to be genuinely different. And this new woman kept pressing me with questions."

Adam read the rain's trickling script on the front windshield. "You thought she was out to undermine you with your father. This strange woman who had inserted herself into your father's life while you were away."

Kayla stared at the rain and whispered, "I'm so ashamed."

"I've only met Honor that one time. But it's enough to know she hasn't just forgiven you. She's forgotten it."

Adam knew she wanted to brush his words aside. So he was up and moving before she could respond. He stepped into the rain and firmly shut the door. Moved to the trunk and pulled out his battered grip. Went back to the driver's door and watched her slip over the middle divider and start the car.

He gently touched her shoulder. "Thank you for helping me with this, Kayla. It means more than you will ever know."

She closed the door, then sat and stared at him, a bleak look through the rain. He smiled once more and planted his fingers upon the side window, right at the level of her lips.

chapter 15

*A*dam changed clothes and called his mother while standing by his bedroom window. From her first word, he knew it was
not a good day. He stifled his worries and his own need to talk, as
he had on so many other such times. A few words of reassurance
was all he permitted himself, only the things that would ease her
through this bad time. He then dialed the nurses' station from
memory. The hospice aides all knew him, knew where he was,
and treated him gently. No, nothing new. Just a bad day. Yes, of
course they would phone if there was any change. Adam gave
them his new cell-phone number as a contact and asked that they
pass it on to his mother.

He slipped the phone into his pocket and raised the tall
sash window as far as it would go. He stood close enough for
the rain to dampen his face. But his breath did not come any
easier.

From the floor below came strident calls of farewell. Children
shrieked and thundered along the downstairs hallway. Doors
were slammed, first in the house and then in a car out front. The
silence afterward was deafening.

Adam descended the stairs and knocked on the parlor's

closed door. At the sound of the faint voice within, he opened and asked, "Do you mind some more company?"

"Do I mind? My dear young man, there is no harsher hour to my week than the endless minutes after my family departs. Come in, come in. I fear you shall need to make your own tea, as Mrs. Brandt is off visiting her own children."

"I'm fine, thanks."

"My son and daughter-in-law want me to come live with them. But my dear late husband is here, do you see. He positively adored this old place. I fear were I to leave, I would lose this final shred of his company." She waited until Adam was seated in the horsehair chair across from her to inquire, "Does that sound quite mad?"

"To be honest, everything about love strikes me as borderline insane."

"Does it indeed?" A slender cane of wood the color of frozen honey leaned against the arm of her chair. Sylvia Beachley reached over and began rubbing the ivory head. "Now what, may I ask, would bring you to say such a thing?"

"I'm an analyst. A good one. I sift through information. I find patterns. I determine a course that reduces risk and points toward a winning solution."

"Ah. Risk. A winning formula. How very interesting."

"When it comes to love, though, I can't work out a perspective that makes sense. Even when I say what feels most right, even when I do what feels best, I still walk away feeling . . ."

"Wronged. Damaged. Vulnerable. Wounded." Dr. Beachley stroked the cane's head for a long moment, then said, "The tutorial system followed at Oxford is a most curious practice. The tutor's task is not to help students graduate or increase their grades. It is to prepare them for *life*. To help them identify core issues, such as what their gifts are, where their passions lie, and how they might make the most of the days they have here on earth. There are certain rules which dominate a tutorial. One, there is no wrong question. Two, whatever the course, the student commits to accepting the challenge and studying. Studying hard."

"Is that what we're having? A tutorial?"

"That is for you to determine, young man."

"I'd like that a lot."

"How very interesting. Do you know, I've recently been presented with quite a serious dilemma from another of my students. One to which you may very well hold the key. I have been sitting here wondering whether you came here for this reason, as it were. But an issue of trust is involved, and I have wondered . . . But all that in due course." She thumped her cane. "Very well. Young man, the first rule of analysis, then, is to *determine your parameters*. Do you understand this term, *parameters*?"

"Borders. Boundaries."

"Precisely. You must define the structure within which you operate. There must be limitations, assumptions, givens. But with love, what can these be? How can you establish the proper dimensions of affection?"

"Experience."

"Experience is decidedly the crucial aspect which most affects our self-determination. But what if the experience of love is bad? What if all we know of past love is pain?"

Adam did not feel what he would have expected, which was, to flee. The professor did not pry. She did not claw at his memories. Nor did she ask him to dump the issues in her lap. It was an astonishing sensation, being stripped until he sat there, emotionally naked, without pain or shame. "Then love becomes something to avoid."

She thumped her cane upon the floor. "Very good. So in this case, the parameters within which we operate are solitude. Isolation. Aloofness. An emotional vacuum. But then arises a stimulus from *outside the parameters*. Suddenly the observer is faced with a calamity. What if the parameters are wrong? What if the defining factors that have ruled a lifetime of research and work and action are totally invalid? What then?"

"I don't know that they're wrong." Adam's voice sounded raw to his own ears.

"No, certainly not. There is always the chance that the *experiment* was wrong. That factors unrelated to the correctness have entered in. The controls were breached."

For some reason, the words rocked him. Not what she had said. But what she implied. "Control."

Dr. Beachley directed her smile at the cane's head. "Oh, I say. You *are* good." She thumped her cane a second time, a gentle drumbeat that reverberated at the core of his being. "For the sake of argument, just for a moment, let us say that the issue we face is indeed that the parameters are flawed. That in order to proceed to the correct analysis, the entire course of study must be changed. This would mean even the most basic of issues are open to change, would it not? Even the *definitions* we have developed, concepts like *risk* and *winning*."

She twisted her head so that she could elevate her gaze to his. "What then, Master Wright? How, then, shall you seek *new* parameters?"

He was silent.

"It would mean looking *beyond* yourself, would it not? Seeking *outside* your experiences."

Adam did not speak.

"But how is this possible? Who are we to trust with such a vital issue as defining the concepts, the core structures, that shape our lives?"

Her gaze was milky with age, her voice cracked and seamed as her face. Yet the power, the sheer brute force, held him captivated. Speechless.

"This, then, is your first assignment, young man. If you are to search beyond your experiences, where should you look? Who could you possibly trust enough to help you define what love is, whether it is worth the *risk* of loving, how you might *win* at this most daunting of challenges?"

Kayla arrived to find the house silent. A note from Honor was propped on the kitchen cabinet, saying her father had been called to an urgent meeting, and Honor had driven him for moral support. Kayla placed Adam's thistles in a tiny crystal vase and reread the note. Honor's concern for Peter came through loud and clear. Kayla unpacked, napped, and returned downstairs in time to watch the early winter dusk take control of the Cotswold valley. The rain had stopped while she slept, and a pale light bathed the dew-soaked world. Kayla's gaze gradually shifted from farmhouse smoke rising in feather-strokes to her own reflection. Memories of her first meeting with Honor misted the rain-streaked glass. She used the ringing phone to turn away.

Adam asked, "Am I calling at a bad time?"

"Hi. No, it's fine."

"I've been downstairs talking with the professor. And something she said . . . Kayla, you need to apologize to Honor. Today."

Kayla carried the phone into the kitchen. She touched the thistles he had given her. Just like the previous day, his sense of timing held a soul-piercing strength.

"Are you there?"

"Yes."

"You just go to her and you say the words."

She set the mug back on the shelf. "I don't have any. Words."

"You mean, you don't have the ones to make the mistake never have happened." Adam gave her space to argue, then continued, "If she's the woman I think she is, whatever you offer will be fine. Because it won't be the words at all. And as far as she's concerned, the mistake is already long gone."

Kayla turned back to the rear windows. The vista beyond

was now lost to the night. She shivered with the realization that this was real. That she could no more run from him now than run from herself.

She heard a soft tapping and knew he was pacing. His footsteps formed a cadence to his words. Kayla found her gaze tracking back and forth across the empty kitchen, as though following his motions.

Adam said, "When Mom got sick, I became eaten up by my own helpless fury. Week by week I watched everything I'd worked for, all my savings, all my *dreams*, just drain away. Mom must have known how angry I was. But she never said anything except to thank me."

His confession drew the night into a parchmentlike fragility. Kayla stepped to the rear window. She stared at the blank glass, willing herself to ask the question, Why was he telling her this? Her fingers tapped against the glass in time to his unseen tread. She did not ask the question. She already knew the answer.

"I'm the worst person in the world to talk about love, Kayla. But I know there are some people out there who have a better handle on it than I ever will. My mom, for one. Not long back I came into her room, and she was doing so bad I was afraid that visit might end up being our last time together. That night I apologized for being a shallow soul. That's what I called myself. Mom smiled and said she was glad I was her son, and that she was proud of me. Three days later, I met your father. He offered me the job. I thanked him and turned him down and had to tell him why. But when I told Mom, she said it was time. And that night she had her first dream and said I'd come over and find the signs. And if I searched, I'd also find the answer for why I had to leave. Mom said it was her final request. I left because I couldn't refuse her anything. Not even if it meant leaving her alone."

"Adam . . ."

"There are a lot of mistakes you can't undo, Kayla. Those are the tragedies. This problem with Honor is bad only so long as you leave it hanging. That's why I called. To tell you to do this now. Tonight. For Honor. For your father. And especially for yourself."

chapter 16

The next morning, Adam sat with his back to the corporate world. He occupied a space he intended to make his own for as long as the company let him stay. The upstairs floor for junior analysts was a difficult place these days. That morning Adam scoured the building, searching for a place that might become truly his, where he could hunker down and focus.

The old manor's central library was tall and narrow and lined on three sides by an open gallery. Downstairs, the central open space contained a table that ran the library's entire thirty-foot length. The upstairs gallery contained three alcoves connected to the main floor by a trio of circular staircases. Each alcove contained a table, reading lights, and two chairs. The surrounding floor-to-ceiling bookshelves were full of leather-backed volumes. The space suited him perfectly.

Adam spaced his charts and computer around the table, claiming his territory. He leafed through a stack of articles he had downloaded. He labeled a trio of new folders for investment opportunities that required further study. He stacked the files to one side, took out a legal pad and pen and a fourth empty folder. Adam was a great one for building paper dossiers. He did this for every project he analyzed. He would sketch out half-completed thoughts, then file them away with the news-paper clippings and financial reports and everything else that might prove interesting. Repeatedly he would lay out all the fragments and sort through them, not pressing, just allowing his subconscious to try to form a cohesive reality.

Adam decided to structure the previous day's tutorial in the same manner. It was the only way he could conceive of handling what he faced. Even so, he found it very hard to begin. To write anything meant unraveling the bundle of ten-sion and coming down to the core elements.

His hand remained poised over the file's label. What was he to call it?

He finally wrote the word, *Parameters*.

He stared at it for a very long time, recalling the professor's soft voice, the parlor's gray light, the rain, the impact of her words. He had woken up that morning knowing with utter certainty that he needed to reexamine all the issues shaping his world. Look at them one by one. Only by separating them out could he hope to make any sense of the tumult.

He started two lists on the page. One was business, the other personal. But he found himself unable to divide up the issues. Where was he to put his mother's dreams? He was seated here in this company library because of them. And Kayla? Did he sepa-rate her from her project? If so, what about his offer to invest her project's funds? Adam tore out the sheet and started a new page, one where everything was listed together. It was utterly illogical to line up the emotional with the financial. It defied everything he had sought to do with his life. This became the echoing refrain as he took the main points and began drawing trees out to the right of each word, adding further details, watching the lines of tension fill the page. His entire life had been spent isolating his emotions from his work. Denying his memories. Ignoring his need for others. And where had it brought him? Adam stopped and stared at the sheet in front of him. The page was a jumbled torrent of words and risks and crossed lines of tension. There was no sense to it. None at all.

The ringing sound was so unfamiliar it took him a moment to recognize it as his new cell phone. He dug the phone from his jacket pocket and pressed the connect button.

The security consultant Peter Austin had recommended sounded as crisp and official as he had on Saturday morning. But his voice also contained a note of genuine triumph.

Adam felt the detective's words strike with the force of a hammer. "Repeat that again."

As the detective went over his findings a second time, Adam watched the lines he had drawn on the sheet of paper begin to unfurl. One by one, they straightened and came together in perfect harmony.

It was only when he hung up the phone that he realized someone was calling his name. "Up here."

Joshua Dobbins paraded up the stairs. The finance chief wore his trademark dark gray suit and overly narrow tie. The alcove's shadows deepened the acne scars on his cheeks. He sneered at Adam. "I see you've been nesting. What a pity."

Adam nodded slowly, so captured by what he had just learned he felt utterly insulated from what was about to come. "You got your way with the board."

Dobbins flushed angrily. "Apparently Peter unwisely chose to bandy about confidential information. Which only adds to my pleasure in dismissing you."

"On what grounds?"

"Spare us the need to prolong this, Wright. As you have not even signed a contract, I see no need for complaint."

"There's something you should know—"

"Oh, please. You don't actually think I might have the slightest interest in some further analysis."

Adam tore the sheet from the notebook and started to fold it. "You never can tell."

"No you don't!" Joshua reached over and tore the page from Adam's hand. "You take nothing from this company, do you hear me? Nothing at all. You are fired. Axed. No longer welcome." Dobbins spun about, walked to the railing, and said to the security guard below, "Escort this gentleman from the premises."

When Kayla came downstairs that morning, she discovered Honor seated at the kitchen table. Her forehead rested on one hand. The fingers of her other hand traced a line in the wood's grain. "Is everything all right?"

Honor took her time responding. "Not really, no."

"Is it Daddy?"

"Partly." Honor used both hands to sweep her hair away from her face. "I need to do something this morning. But I don't want to, and to be perfectly honest I'm not quite sure if I even can."

Kayla leaned against the kitchen cabinet. "That makes two of us."

"Excuse me?"

She took a very hard breath and launched straight in. "I need to apologize. And not because Daddy asked me to. Because I was wrong in how I thought about you. And how I responded to your questions about . . ."

"That horrid man," Honor said quietly. "Geoffrey."

"Right. Him. And I'm especially, extremely sorry for not being here when you got married. All the reasons I had for not returning, every single one, were wrong."

Honor sat with her back to the winter valley and the gray blanket overhead. For once, Honor did not touch her belly. It was a habit Honor had, whenever she was troubled or worried. Shielding the child with one or both hands. Only now Honor sat and watched Kayla with a calm intensity. Both hands remained flat on the table between them. "You are an answer to one woman's very desperate prayers."

"That was not exactly the response I was expecting."

"No?"

"A bit of vindication, maybe. A quick little dab with the paring knife."

"Kayla, please."

"It's what I deserve."

"If we all got what we deserve, we'd be doomed." She came slowly to her feet. "I must tell you, your speaking with me just now is a gift. I am dreading something, but I have to do it, and I don't want to do it on my own. Will you come with me, please?"

"Sure."

"I must warn you, it could be most unpleasant."

Kayla pushed away from the counter, feeling weightless from having the apology behind them both. "Let's roll."

Her father's wife drove a silver gumdrop of a car. Honor drove into Oxford with tightfisted tension, her normally placid face creased in worry. Kayla held her silence until they were seated in a café on Little Clarendon Street, a narrow lane running between the colleges and the surrounding businesses. "Why are we here?"

"I am supposed to meet my sister." Honor glanced at her watch. "She's late. She may not come at all. She hates me."

Kayla realized just how little she knew about her father's wife. "I find that a little hard to believe."

"Emily loathes me and always has. Peter won't allow her into our home. This morning he refused point-blank to come with me." Honor rubbed her swollen belly. "I feel so vulnerable now."

"Daddy won't let her in the house?"

"I know that doesn't sound like Peter. But it's true." Honor jerked at the ringing of the bell over the door. She sighed, partly with disappointment, partly from relief. "If Emily does come, it will be because she needs money."

The bell tinkled, and Honor jerked once more. Kayla felt her own tension rising. "Why do you do it?"

"Peter asks me the same thing. And the answer is, I feel I must."

Kayla leaned across the table. "You're not alone in this."

Honor's eyes were impossibly big. "Thank you for coming, Kayla."

"Tell me about your family."

"There's just Emily and Momma close by now. My mother is in a nursing home and has forbidden me from ever coming to visit her again."

The news pushed Kayla back in her chair. "Why?"

"Because I spoke to her about my faith. Or tried to. I have a brother, Drew. But he immigrated to South America when I was nine. With my father. They live in Bogotá. Or they did. I haven't heard from either in years. My father was a school headmaster. He was caught having an affair with a fifteen-year-old student. The scandal cost my father his job. We also lost our home, since we lived in the headmaster's residence. After living on the dole for a year, my father fled to Colombia."

The bell rang once more, and this time Honor's entire body went rigid. "Here she is."

Honor's sister wore clothes that made a statement of angry disdain. Her hat was a knit glove that mashed her hair and elongated her angular face. From the back of the cap grew a squirrel's tail. Her dress was the color of dried mud. Over it she wore a black lumpish cloak knotted at her neck. "Well,

well. How quaint. What do they say these days? It used to be a bun in the oven."

"Hello, Emily." Honor's voice had gone still as a winter's dusk. "This is Kayla, Peter's daughter."

"That would make you a pregnant bride and a stepmother to boot." She unfastened her cloak, draped it over the chair. "How utterly domestic."

Kayla asked, "Can I get you something?"

"I won't be staying. Wouldn't want to disturb my sister's tranquillity." Tight lips were painted a Chinese-lacquer red. The color accentuated their twisted slant, as though Emily chewed constantly on the inside of her left cheek. "Kayla, is it? So how do you feel about having a stepmother who's scarcely older than you?"

"I'm utterly delighted." Kayla took a firm hold on Honor's hand. "As long as it's Honor."

Emily sat sideways, her chin far too high, her arm slung over her cloak, her hand limp. "Can I smoke in here?"

Honor replied, "You know you can't."

"The nanny state. How revolting. Never mind. So how is the old gentleman. Getting around all right, despite his advanced years?"

"Peter is fine."

"Still keeping you happy, I suppose. Living in your sweet little country villa, lording it over the rest of us."

"Emily, please."

"Really, Honor. The man is old enough to be your grandfather." Her gaze was as compressed as her lips, as though staring through perpetually burning smoke. The eyes glinted as she asked Kayla, "Did my perfect darling of a sister tell you about our little family drama?"

"Yes. I'm sorry."

Emily sniffed. "When you next hear from Papa, do give him my best, will you?"

Honor used her free hand to reach inside her purse and came out with an envelope. "I can't manage to offer you as much as last year."

"Things a bit tight, are they?"

"Yes. Merry Christmas, Emily."

"Oh, my, it must be ever so hard, running an estate on the allowance his lordship provides." Emily redirected her smirk at Kayla's grip on Honor's hand. "How sweet. My dear sister has made a new friend."

Kayla tightened her grip. "That's right. She has."

They left the café as soon as they could be certain not to run into Emily. On the walk back to Honor's car, Kayla's anger cooled to confusion. She had not given much thought to Honor's background. But if she had, Kayla would have assumed the lady came from a perfect family. A home where values were locked in early and well, where love was taught by example, where tragedies were of a manageable size. Certainly not this—father disgraced, family torn apart, loved ones scattered across the world, embittered remnants sniping at each over, jealous of every crumb.

Honor unlocked the door and slipped behind the wheel. She started the car, turned the heat up full, slipped off her gloves, and rubbed her hands together. "Seeing Emily always leaves me feeling like I've been frozen to the core."

"She's horrid."

"I'm sorry you had to meet her. But I'm glad you came. It means so much, you just can't imagine."

Honor spoke the words to the front windshield. Which gave Kayla the chance to study the woman seated beside her. She would have liked to put Honor's character down to some wayward gene, some chance happening at a molecular level that left Honor with a saintly disposition and the ability to endure such an attack without anger of her own. "You two could not be more different."

"I have nightmares." Honor blew on her hands and rubbed them again. "I wake up next to your father and discover I'm Emily."

"That couldn't happen," Kayla said firmly. "Not in a million years."

"I dream there's some part of her that crawls up into my brain and takes over. I snip at him and he looks at me with that look of gentle confusion. And I wake up weeping because I've hurt a very good man."

"Daddy is so lucky to have you."

Honor's eyes grew round. She blinked fiercely, but one tear managed to escape. She whispered, "I'm so worried about him. And the company."

"I know. Me too."

"It means everything to him."

Kayla smiled sadly. "Not everything. Not by a long shot."

"I wish I could do something . . ."

Kayla reached over and embraced the woman. The gear-shift jammed into her thigh, and their bulky coats made it hard to take a full grip. Kayla said, "You do more for Daddy than you will ever know."

They remained like that for a moment, long enough for all the mistakes to evaporate.

Honor finally straightened, wiped her face with both hands, then fumbled inside her purse. "I promised Peter I'd phone as soon as we were done."

Kayla leaned back and straightened her coat and smoothed her hair. Normal motions of a normal day. Two women seated in a car heated against the cold, out for a morning errand. Friends.

Honor said, "That's impossible."

"What?"

"I have twelve messages." Honor pressed the key, held the phone to her ear, gasped.

"What's the matter?"

Honor dropped the phone to her lap, slapped the car into gear, and said, "Something terrible has happened."

chapter 17

Kayla found Adam seated behind the wheel of her father's car in the company lot. Several sheets of paper were spread across the seat next to him. A black rubbish bag was dumped on the rear seat. A neighboring tree rustled overhead, a gentle sound, light as laughter. Adam scribbled furiously, not looking up until she opened his door. He greeted her with, "Joshua fired me."

"I know. I'm so sorry it's taken this long. Honor and I . . . We came as soon as we heard."

"It's okay. Your father let me wait here so I wouldn't freeze."

Kayla inspected him for gaping wounds. Adam did not sound cheerful. But not unhappy either. Kayla stated what she and Honor had decided was the best course of action. "I'm taking you home."

"Can't." He tore the sheet from his notebook and started working on the next. "We've got work to do."

"Honor will come back for Daddy. Move over, I'll drive."

"We're not going to your house." He began gathering notes. "We're going to London."

Kayla protested, "They just dumped you on the street."

"On the drive, actually. But never mind."

"Never mind? That's all you can say?"

"Actually, I have quite a lot more to tell you. But not here."

"You're not making any sense."

"I know. There's something we have to do. Together." He gathered his papers off the seat. "We need to hurry."

Kayla drove them downtown and parked in the lot across from Oxford's central train station. They made the next high-speed service with seconds to spare. Adam slipped into a seat opposite hers, spread out his papers on the table between them, and went back to work. Kayla assumed he had a job interview lined up. Perhaps her father had arranged something for him. She repressed the urge to pry. She was certain she would find out soon enough. For the moment, she was grateful for a fragment of time to sort through the morning's events.

Honor was a woman of grace and a giving heart. She loved her new husband and blessed their home with love and peace. These were not imaginings. Kayla could not argue with this. Yet the facts and the woman stood in direct contrast to what Kayla had just witnessed. Honor came from a world of bitterness and abandonment and hurt. Kayla knew there was a unique message there. She knew this, and she was frightened by the knowledge. Because if it could happen to Honor, why not to her? Yet to accept this as a possibility meant giving in to the most painful thought of all.

Hope.

While Adam remained absorbed in his work, she studied

him. He stopped writing and sorted his notes. He flattened the creases and rubbed away the folds. He lined the pages like soldiers about the narrow table. When there was not enough room, he handed Kayla her purse without looking up. She touched his fingers when she took her purse and absorbed an electric shock in the process. Adam did not notice either the touch or her shiver. The outside world was gone to him now. He did not hear the train rock through a village station or the whistle. Nothing interrupted his concentration, not even her inspection.

London grew up around their train in a jumbled fashion, soot-stained and graffiti-scarred. Only in the distance could there be seen a few hints of the glory beyond the city's blemished outskirts. Adam sighed and straightened in his seat. He glanced out the window. There was no sky worth a mention, just a flat city grayness. When Adam turned back, Kayla said, "I spoke with Honor this morning. And apologized. You were right."

Adam nodded slowly. "This is important. And I want to hear all about it. But not right now, okay?"

"What is it, Adam?"

He kept nodding as the train pulled into Paddington Station. "Soon. Very soon."

They took a taxi. Adam read an address off his notes, a street she did not recognize. She gave name to a few of the sights they passed—Hyde Park, Marble Arch, Piccadilly, the Ritz, Buckingham Palace. Christmas lights flickered overhead. Wreaths hung from numerous front doors. Adam watched the city scene with silent intensity.

Kayla reached over and straightened his tie. "Is it just like you imagined?"

"To be honest, there's so much going on right now I wonder if I'll remember anything I'm seeing."

"Can you at least tell me where we're going?"

"The security firm your dad put us onto."

"They've found something?"

"Maybe." He held up his hand. "I really need you to wait, okay?"

The security firm was located on Linacre Lane, a dingy street of prewar brick and grime. As they started down the alley, Big Ben struck the hour from a very long block away. The corporate security firm and detective agency occupied the building's entire ground floor. Adam gave his name to the receptionist, then stood by the front doors. Kayla could feel the tension radiating off him in waves. She wanted to ask why he was so abuzz about something related to the firm that just fired him. But he had asked her to wait. It was not in her nature to be patient or to relinquish control. Especially to a man. But the morning's journey with Honor remained a vivid component of the day.

The man who approached was in his mid-thirties and both muscled and lean. His pin-striped suit was wrinkled from too many wears between cleanings. "Mr. Wright?"

"Yes." Adam shook the offered hand. "This is Kayla Austin."

"Good of you to come. William Foley, senior security consultant. Shall we go back?"

The security agent, a title he preferred over private detective, went by Bill. He hoped one day to enter Scotland Yard. But in the meantime, doing corporate security work wasn't a bad gig for a man desperate to escape the provinces. He had previously done a stint in the forces as an MP with the Royal Gloucesters, and straight up, the life wasn't nearly so bad as what people on the outside might think. All this was given in a nervous rush as they walked back to his cubicle. When they were seated and had declined the agent's offer of tea, Foley asked Adam, "How do you want this to play out?"

Adam turned to Kayla, a serious look on his face. "I need you to look at a couple of photos."

She knew. Before she asked, she knew the answer. Adam's dark gaze held enough focused intensity for her to ask, "It's Geoffrey, isn't it? You've found him."

Adam said to Foley, "Show her."

The agent slid the single file on his desk over in front of her. "Bit grainy, these. Shot in fairly awful light yesterday evening. Couldn't use a flash, of course. But they should do for the process of identification. Or elimination."

Kayla watched her hand reach out. The folder's cover held a delicate sensation, like very old dirt. She opened it. And gasped.

"The bloke's name is Steen. Derek Steen." A note of pride entered the agent's voice. "Soon as I spotted him, I knew it was our man."

It was the first time she had seen his image in months. The yellow streetlight and the photo's grainy quality turned him sallow and dug caverns below his jaw.

Adam asked, "Is it him?"

Kayla swallowed, but the breath was not there for a response. She turned to the next photo. Geoffrey spoke to someone cropped from the picture. His smile reached out and gripped her gut. Kayla put a hand to her mouth, clamping down on a sudden wave of nausea.

"Kayla?"

She released her mouth and gripped the arm of the chair. "It's him."

The agent asked, "What's he done, then?"

When Kayla did not respond, Adam said, "He stole six hundred thousand pounds from a project she ran."

Kayla looked at Adam. "Everything. He took everything."

Adam asked the detective, "Do we still have time?"

Foley glanced at his watch. "Should just make it. If we can snag a taxi, that is."

Adam rose from his chair. "You heard the man. We need to hurry."

"We're leaving?"

Adam spoke with the gentle firmness of a man dealing with the recently bereaved. "There's more, Kayla."

They left the security firm and took a taxi into the City, site of Roman Londinium, still bordered by fragments of the ancient wall, and which now housed the financial district. Adam had heard of the City all his professional life. He had once dreamed of working here, his abilities recognized by the financial world.

Deal in hundreds of millions of pounds or euros or dollars, the fate of corporations teetering on the phone in his hand. Billing out at thousands of dollars an hour, being courted by industrial kings, so keen an analyst he was able to remain independent and sell his services to the highest bidder. Suits by Saville Row, wheels by Lamborghini, plane by Gulfstream, home by Berkeley Square. A winner.

Instead, he sat on a little fold-down seat and faced out the taxi's rear window. He held the detective's video camera in his lap. Kayla sat across from him, glancing over every now and then. But most of her attention was captured by the manila folder that Bill Foley, the detective, held in his lap. Bill sat next to Kayla and gabbed on about how rare it was in his trade to come up with the goods in less than two days.

They rolled down the long Goswell Road corridor, with the Barbican's windowless ground floor barricade to one side and a hodgepodge of cheerless buildings on the other. The taxi swung past Saint Paul's Cathedral and the Guildhall and entered a different realm, one liberally slathered with money. The people were flash, the buildings rich, the tempo frenetic. The City was the world's most powerful center for international finance, surpassing even New York and Tokyo. A place Adam had always dreamed of entering one day.

They pulled up in front of a new building fashioned of cream-colored tile and dark smoked glass. Kayla read the name emblazoned in bronze above the entrance and cried, "But we can't come here!"

Adam felt his entire body quivering with a tension he only

half understood. Even so, his voice held to its steady calm. "We have to."

"But . . . This is Madden and Van Pater headquarters!"

"I realize that, Kayla."

Her features were tightly pinched. "You don't understand. You can't. They've hounded Daddy for years!"

Adam leaned forward and took hold of her hand. "I know this is hard for you, Kayla. But we have *got* to do this."

"This is so not good. Daddy would explode if he heard."

"We'll tell him tonight and see, but I think he'll tell you we did the right thing."

"That's impossible."

"This is the company your father thinks is trying to sink his ship, right?"

"He and Joshua both."

"Can you give me some details?"

Kayla looked out the front window. "While he was still working for them, Daddy started making inroads with the Oxford colleges and their endowment programs. He went to the MVP board and asked them to set up an Oxford office. He said the university required a different approach from the normal City edict of profit above all else. He said this new office should be quasi-independent, allowed to take an altogether different approach."

"But MVP refused your father, didn't they?" Adam filled in the blanks. "So Peter quit the company, started up his own group, and made a success of it. And they've been after him ever since."

She shuddered. "We have to leave here, Adam."

"Kayla, listen to me. This is going to be hard for you. But

we're after solving a problem. A very serious crisis. And we can only do this with your help." He turned to the detective and asked, "How much longer?"

Bill Foley glanced at his watch. "Any moment now. According to the lass I spoke with, you could set your watch by this bloke. By all accounts he's a work hard, play harder type. Him and his pack, they go to that champagne bar you see round the corner there. Leave the premises bang on time, claim the same table every day. Leastwise, that's what I was told."

Kayla looked from one man to the other. "Who?"

Adam made sure the video was up and running. His fingers were trembling slightly, but his voice remained steady. "Watch closely."

Bill pointed out the window. "That's him coming out of the front doors now."

Adam held back just far enough to ensure the taxi's shadows hid his camera. He was amazed at how calm he felt. Tremors touched his viewfinder every now and then. Even so, far more than the camera's lens detached him from everything going on out there on the street. And even here inside the taxi. He heard Kayla's sharp intake of breath. Beside her on the seat, the detective said, "Best stay back, miss. Don't want him seeing you now, do we?"

"This can't be happening!"

Adam zoomed in more tightly on the man walking down the sidewalk on the other side of the street. The camera went out of focus, then sharpened. Adam was grateful for this distance, very grateful indeed. "That's him, isn't it? Geoffrey. The thief."

chapter 18

*A*dam had never had much contact with American cops. But he suspected they held a lot of similarities to their British counterparts. They were seated in an office on the third floor of the new Scotland Yard headquarters. Outside the window to the right of his chair, Adam could see the red buses trundle past, the black humpbacked taxis, the white-stoned buildings of ancient London town. The two policemen seated across from them were members of the Fraud Squad. Their accents were clipped, their uniforms and badges distinctly British. But they gave Kayla the same flat cop-gaze. And they responded with the same blunt directness.

The male policeman occupied the chair behind the desk. "I'm afraid there is very little we can do for you, Miss Austin."

"I'm handing him to you on a plate," Kayla protested.

"Hardly that. You are describing a crime that took place on the soil of a different sovereign nation."

"Involving money from a British trust."

The younger of the two officers, a dark-haired woman who

made up for her diminutive stature with a rock-solid density, said, "She has a point."

The male officer gave her a sour look. "The crime took place in Kenya."

"Tanzania," Kayla corrected. "We operate in both countries, but our central office—"

"Kenya, Tanzania, Timbuktu, the result is the same insofar as this office is concerned. The crime took place outside our jurisdiction."

The female officer, however, was a trifle more sympathetic. "We could send a flyer to the local authorities."

"That won't help us," Kayla said glumly. "They lost interest in Geoffrey's theft the moment they heard everything was taken. Which meant there was nothing left to bribe them with."

The male officer checked his notes. "I thought you said his name was Derek."

"It was. Is. But I knew him as Geoffrey."

The officer started to make a note, but thought better of it and set down his pen. "That changes nothing so far as we are concerned."

"But—"

"Let's just review what we have, shall we?" He glanced at his associate, clearly arguing with her as well. "This Derek or Geoffrey was hired by your organization. He worked with you for, how long was it?"

"About six months."

"He then left. At the same time, your bank account and your office safe were both allegedly cleaned out."

"There's no *alleged* about this!"

"We have nothing except your word to go on here, Miss Austin. And even if we accept that a crime took place, we have no way to tie him to this." Another look at his associate, then he added, "As far as we are concerned, you might have stolen the funds yourself."

Kayla turned bitter. "From my own father?"

"It's happened before. Six hundred thousand pounds is a substantial sum."

"Then why would I have come in here?"

Adam spoke for the first time since entering the office. "Thanks for seeing us. Come on, Kayla. We're all done here."

The female officer accompanied them back to the elevators. She introduced herself as Inspector Walton, pushed the elevator button, and said, "I for one accept that a genuine crime was committed."

Kayla was evidently too hot from the exchange to respond. So Adam said, "Thank you."

"My children insist on eating Fair Trade produce every chance they get. I admire you for what you've tried to do." She handed Adam her card. "If you can come up with anything concrete that ties this character to the deed, do please let me know."

On the train back to Oxford, Kayla flashed continually back to the shocking moments. In the early days, her parents had often spoken of MVP's tactics. How they were bent on destroying her father's new company. How nothing was too low for them.

And now this. Geoffrey Rambling, the man she assumed was lost and gone forever. Walking down the sidewalk, flashing his pirate's grin at the people to either side. The man in control. The winner.

The only thing that kept her anchored to earth was Adam's hand. He sat beside her and did not speak. One hand was entwined around hers, the other rested on the seat behind her head. She felt his warmth and strength radiating out, enveloping her. Giving her the ability to draw the world back into focus and say, "I want to kill him."

Adam did not speak. His dark gaze held coppery glints of light. He watched her with an unblinking calm.

"Find a gun, walk up to him, let him get a good look at who it is, and bang. Finished."

Adam held her gaze and remained silent.

"Don't you have anything to say?"

"I'm waiting."

"For what?"

"For you to get over the shock and come back to earth."

"You don't think I'm serious?"

"I know it's not going to happen. And so do you."

She turned to the window. The train passed a bend in the river Thames. A village of thatched houses and open timbers passed by. The winter waters were still and slate gray, the party boats gone for the season. "How can you be so calm?"

"I had a couple of hours to work through it before you arrived. And I wasn't the one he stole from." Adam paused, then added, "At least, not directly."

Kayla felt a hint of warmth touch a spot that had been frozen since seeing Geoffrey's photograph. She did not care what name the detective might give to the thief. To her, he remained Geoffrey Rambling, the man who used his looks and his smile to lie and steal and destroy.

She said, "I have to tell Daddy."

"Not yet."

"What?"

"He's still at the office. The company is still in crisis mode. And I've been fired, remember?"

Kayla glanced at her watch. It was not yet four o'clock. Which was impossible. The day already seemed eons in length.

Adam said, "On the way out, you said you'd spoken with Honor."

"I don't want to talk about that now. I can't."

"Just tell me this. Was I right to call and speak with you like I did?"

She wanted to push it away. Her mind was too full. But Adam's face was tense with an expectancy so powerful it looked almost like worry. "Yes. You were."

"Great. That's great."

"What made you say what you did?"

He hesitated a fraction, then replied, "I had a tutorial."

"What?"

Adam said, "It would make more sense if I showed you."

Adam found a spot for her father's big Mercedes just down the road from the boardinghouse where he lived. He sat looking at her reflectively.

"What is it?" she asked.

"I know this has been a really hard day for you."

"You could say that."

"If you want to stay in the car, it's okay. But I'd really like it if you could come in with me."

"You want me to sit in on a tutorial you're having with Dr. Beachley?"

"That's what she calls it."

"What's your name for it, then?"

"All I can tell you is, she makes me think in different ways. Will you come?"

When they entered the front parlor, the professor's delight was evident in her voice. "Young Master Wright. And you brought Kayla. How splendid. I fear you shall need to make your own tea. Mrs. Brandt has gone off to do some Christmas shopping for her grandchildren."

"We don't need anything."

"Stuff and nonsense. It will do us all a world of good. You know where everything is, Master Wright."

Adam sounded oddly formal. "I'd appreciate it if you'd call me Adam, ma'am."

"Adam. The good china resides in the cupboard beside the boiler. And see if there's not a fresh packet of Scottish shortbread in the pantry. My dear, perhaps you would be so kind as to turn on a lamp or two. The daylight is failing as fast as my eyes."

Kayla switched on lamps made from whalebone and bronze. The light formed golden islands in a room of shadows and soft edges. The world beyond the gauze curtains was dappled gray.

"That's much better. Come sit down and tell me how you are."

Kayla took the horsehair chair opposite the round side table from the professor. "The day has been incredible."

"I take it from your expression that this incredibleness is not altogether good."

"No."

"Nor welcome."

"That's a harder one."

The professor reached over and patted her hand. "My dear, I wish I could tell you what it means to have you sit here with me. It is as though my fondest recollections have grown wings and flown into the present to keep me company."

Kayla found the internal tumult calming somewhat. "Mother loved coming to see you. I remember when it was cold outside, you let me sit at your table and color in my books."

Dr. Beachley cleared a corner of one eye. "You were such a dear child. And so very much like your mother. The resemblance was quite astonishing. Then and now." Dr. Beachley beamed as Adam brought in a tray. "How nice. I'm sure your young man has prepared a splendid tea."

Kayla felt an automatic desire to reject the words *your young man*. Especially today. But she remained silent as Adam set the tray on the table between them. He served tea to the ladies, then drew over a chair and poured another cup. By then it was too late, the words drifting in the parlor's cozy atmosphere.

Your young man.

The professor asked Adam, "Have you been working on your topic, young man?"

"Yes." Adam drew out the yellow sheets from his jacket pocket. He unfolded them carefully. "I'm not done yet."

"With such questions, the answers may require a lifetime to be fully realized." Her demeanor had altered subtly. The professor accepted the pages and set them on the table beside the tray. "I shall inspect these later. Can you summarize your findings for me?"

"I had to split the issue," Adam replied. "First I needed to figure out how I got the initial parameters so wrong."

"Not wrong, young man. Merely flawed. You did the best you could at the time. But you have grown *beyond* where you were. You now recognize your initial boundaries as inadequate. You seek to *redraw* your parameters. Correct?"

"Yes."

"So. Flawed how?"

Adam set his cup back on the tray and bundled his hands into his lap. "I established parameters for love based on pain. Which meant I assumed love was the same as loss and helplessness and rage."

"I don't understand." Kayla pointed at the pages on the tray. "All that work you were doing, I thought it was about Geoffrey working for my father's company."

"I don't know how it all fits together. But my gut tells me that it does."

The professor pressed gently, "You were speaking of how you had equated love with pain."

"Not consciously. But that's how I structured my life. I wasn't going to be hurt. So I kept love out."

The professor fumbled in the process of settling her cup on the tray. "So there are two parameters you are now questioning, are there not?"

"That love does not always bring pain." Adam's forehead creased with the effort of seeing the answer. "And I've been wrong to try and remain in total control."

"Oh, I say," the professor murmured. She reached over and gripped the cane leaning against the arm of her chair and began kneading the top. "Well. It would be unrealistic to assume that if you open your heart, your mind, the very essence of your being to another, that you can remain free from pain. Would you not agree?"

Adam rocked the entire upper half of his body. "Yes."

"And yet there is the willingness, at least with some, to *accept* this risk of pain. How is that possible? Whatever would make such a peril worth taking?"

Adam continued to rock. Back and forth. His hands locked in his lap. His gaze inward. Distant.

"So. That is a question for another time. Now, young man. You said you had confronted another issue besides the flawed parameters themselves."

When he cleared his throat, it sounded as though he was

fighting against something locked around his air passage. "I need to figure out how to establish boundaries of love that are based on love, and not on fear. Not on experience. But on hope."

Kayla felt as though she had become locked into an invisible cage. One fashioned by gentle words and a room of soft light and soothing shadows. She wanted to lash out, to remind them of what she had just discovered that day. To draw the discussion back to the jagged edges of a man who stole everything and now worked for her father's enemy.

Instead, she was ensnared by a high-backed chair and a retired professor and a man who rocked now in silence. She wanted to weep, she wanted to reach out and grip this man so hard she could draw the goodness from him. Find in herself the ability to search as he was doing. Because she knew with utter certainty why Adam had wanted her to be with him here. And why he sought these impossible answers.

Impossible that he would ask this of her. To love. To hope. To reach beyond everything she had endured. Even today. Impossible.

Dr. Beachley allowed the silence to blanket them all for a moment, then said, "Knowing the proper question, defining the issue, is the essential element here. You have done a commendable job of that, young man. As I said, the answers may take a lifetime, or they may come with a blinding flash of realization. But you are asking what you must in order to grow beyond the past." Her hands were joined on the cane, softly rubbing the ivory handle. "I would award your first tutorial the highest possible grade."

Adam tasted a smile. His gaze drifted up but did not quite connect with Kayla's. "Thank you."

Dr. Beachley broke the moment by turning and asking, "From your earlier comment, young lady, might I assume there is a different issue than Adam's that has brought you here today?"

Adam looked at her now. "I'll tell her if you want. But I think you should."

"Tell her?"

"About Derek and your project."

"Geoffrey," she corrected faintly.

Adam nodded. "Geoffrey," he agreed.

"So," the professor said. "Now I have two students. How excellent. Some queries proceed so much better if they are shared."

Kayla found no logic whatsoever in speaking about the day with this woman who was a friend of her mother's yet a stranger to her present life. But the act of listening to Adam had left her without the ability to close herself off. What was the word that Adam had used? Parameters. The boundaries of her life had been fractured, such that Kayla found herself relating the day, and then answering further questions about her project and her father's company and their involvement, and the theft. And where she had just come from. And what she had just witnessed. She spoke in parcels that were rather breathless and often not in complete sentences. The professor listened with an intensity matched by the force within Adam's dark gaze.

When Kayla finished, the professor said, "Before Adam's first tutorial, I mentioned a dilemma another of my former students is currently facing. One for which I had no answer save prayer. But what I have heard from you two today, I can only take as a sign that here in this room lies the solution to my former student's problem. She is a biochemist doing quite remarkable research on the eradication of pain. Yet she has been severely scalded by some underhanded dealings." She kneaded the head of her cane, staring into the distance. She then took a long breath and straightened in her chair. "On that matter I must speak with her and come back to you. In the meantime, I shall begin your next assignment by sharing with you a bit of history. The house you see here was purchased with your father's help."

"Daddy never said anything about that."

"Oh, he didn't actually reach into his wallet and hand over the sum required. But my husband and I were working on the question of blood coagulation. They were heady days, so many different issues coming up, the advent of new methods of healing and diagnosis that rocked the foundations of medicine. We met in the lab, two postdoctoral students who were passionate about being at the forefront of this new vanguard. And we made an astonishing discovery. Quite unexpectedly. Really a matter of shared intuition rather than normal scientific procedure."

Adam muttered, "Intuition."

"Value that word most highly, young man. But we shall speak of it another time. For now, yes, my husband-to-be and I made an intuitive leap. And the result was a means by which normal blood coagulation could be halted, such that surgical procedures which up to then had been impossible suddenly became reality." Her seamed features glowed with remembered achievement. "Our new drug became part of the success of early heart transplants."

"What does that have to do with Daddy?"

"Your father was working for this company in London. Our college, Christ Church, was seeking a means by which they could utilize our discoveries. Peter tried to convince his company that they needed to establish a new division, one that would help the Oxford scientists transform research into commercial applications. They refused."

"He left MVP because of you?"

"As I recall, he mentioned numerous conflicts with his employer. But we were certainly one of his first projects. He located a pharmaceutical group that brought our product to market. We used our share of the royalties to purchase this home. We have much to thank your father for, my dear. As does Oxford's scientific community. He went on to establish a system which is still in place today, whereby royalties from such discoveries are shared between the college, the university, the labs, and the scientists."

Adam said, "MVP must have been furious when he left."

"They were livid. Particularly after seven of the colleges shifted their endowment capital to Peter's new company."

Adam leaned back as far as he could without letting go of Kayla's hand. He stared at the ceiling overhead.

Kayla asked, "What is it?"

Adam asked, "What if the guy went down to destroy your project on company orders?"

"What?"

The professor nodded slowly. "I fear you may be onto something there."

"Think about it. Your father's company becomes involved in a project that is helping thousands of poor farmers. The potential PR could be huge. Then what happens but MVP hears about this major potential boost to the company's standing. Joshua claims they've got a spy in the company, right? So MVP sends down Derek Steen with orders to tear your project apart." Adam gave her a tight space, then, "It makes all the sense in the world."

The cane thumped softly upon the floor. "So the assignment has been established. You have a duty to save this good man and his work from corporate oblivion. And I shall do all I can to assist you."

Adam said, "They fired me this morning."

"Oh, stuff and nonsense. What scientist worth his ilk hasn't been faced with potential doom? The occasional setback is to be expected. I would go so far as to suggest that nothing is better for strengthening one's constitution." She leaned heavily upon her cane as she led them toward the door. "Now the pair of you go out there and *achieve.*"

chapter 19

$\mathscr{T}$he final remnants of rush-hour traffic slowed their progress out of Oxford. Night blanketed the world of roads and headlights and half-seen houses. They both remained locked in their respective worlds until they were well past the city's outskirts, when Adam asked, "Did you know about this other part of your father's company?"

Kayla felt as though she were struggling for the surface of roiling internal seas. "I've always known he's been involved in new companies. Once in a while we'd meet the people in Oxford. They were always so excited."

"I've spent my entire life just wanting to be good at this one thing. Then I meet your dad, and he talks my language. But there's so much more to him. He's warm and caring. I see how he is around you and Honor. He may be worn down by this crisis, but he's still got a heart big as England." Adam turned off the main highway and slowed as the hedgerows closed in on either side. "Today I learn about this *other* section of the company. He's not just running a business. He's not just after making the most profit from his capital. He's *helping* people."

"And he likes you."

Adam turned onto the country lane with the river for company. "He makes me feel so small. There are a million people out there doing what I do. Maybe I'm better than most. I think I am. But that possibility doesn't explain why he'd pluck me out of oblivion."

"He sees something in you."

"What? My generosity? My caring nature?"

"You helped your mother."

"I told you. There isn't anybody else. I did it because I had to."

"No, Adam. You said it yourself. You could have run. Why didn't you?"

Adam slowed for the village and turned through the gates. He pulled past the church, parked in front of the house, and cut the motor. "Right after the diagnosis came in, the hospital sat me down and talked about what it was going to cost. Soon as they discovered I didn't have insurance, they gave me both barrels. I went home and packed my suitcases and got online and booked my ticket for Costa. And paced all night. There in the house my mother had made for me, at the cost of all her dreams. I knew that if I left her, I would never be able to live with myself. You can't imagine how trapped I felt, how . . ."

The car was silent except for the ticking clock. Adam finally said, "We have to help him, Kayla. He deserves better than to be taken down by a pirate in a suit. We've got to find a way to stop them. Once and for all."

"How?"

"I don't know. But I know them. Inside MVP are guys just exactly like who I almost became."

Peter Austin greeted them in the front hallway with, "This is an utterly outrageous state of affairs."

Adam suddenly realized, "I took your car."

"Don't be silly, young man. You were welcome to it. I'm speaking about your dismissal." He shuffled ahead of them back toward the kitchen. His breath wheezed slightly as he said, "Joshua and I have had our differences in the past. It's only natural. But he's gone too far this time."

Adam asked, "How many did he let go today?"

"In the end, only you. I phoned the board myself and beseeched them to halt this nonsense before it went any further." He waited while Honor hugged first Kayla and then Adam. Adam felt the bulge of the woman's stomach, the strength of her arms, the concern in her gaze. It only hardened his resolve.

Peter went on, "There's nothing I can do about your own dismissal. Joshua has made it a personal cause."

"It's okay."

"It is anything *but* okay. It is most decidedly *not* okay. I take great umbrage—"

Honor said quietly, "Peter."

He coughed heavily. "Well, really. How can you possibly expect me—"

"Peter, please. They're both exhausted and you sound like

you're coming down with another cold." She asked Kayla, "Have you had anything to eat?"

"No, but that has to wait." She said to her father, "We have something to tell you, Daddy."

Honor protested, "You really must leave whatever it is until tomorrow."

"No," Adam replied. "I'm sorry. But no."

Kayla directed them into seats in front of the television. "It's better if you see this for yourselves. Adam said as much before he told me. And he's right." She slipped the detective's video camera from her purse. "I don't know how to make this work."

"Let me." Adam squatted beside her and began fitting wires. "Okay. Turn on the television."

Peter used the remote. Adam slipped to one side and hit Play. The screen came to life with a slight tremble of the image. Adam heard Kayla's breathing over the microphone. The tension he had felt in the taxi came flooding back. And the disorientation.

Peter exclaimed, "You went to the headquarters of Madden and Van Pater? Today?"

"Wait just a second, Daddy."

Adam heard himself say, "Roll down the window."

Bill Foley's face appeared in the viewfinder. He looked triumphant. Once again he told Kayla to keep well back.

Peter asked, "Who is that man with you?"

"Detective William Foley." Adam's breath was as tight now as in the taxi. "From the security firm you referred me to."

"They've discovered something in two days?"

"Yes. Wait."

The detective said once more, "That's him coming out of the front doors now."

Over the television speakers, Kayla cried aloud. A man appeared, walking down the sidewalk. The camera went fuzzy, then sharpened into vivid clarity. When the man turned toward them and grinned, Adam froze the picture.

"I don't understand," Peter said. "Who are we looking at?"

Adam waited for Kayla to speak. But she sat, stricken and silent, her wounded gaze held by the man with the pirate's smile. "His name is Derek Steen. Otherwise known as Geoffrey Rambling."

Honor gasped and placed both hands protectively over her unborn child.

Peter Austin wheezed, "This can't be."

Adam glanced at Kayla seated on the television's other side. She seemed incapable of speech. "It's him all right."

Peter Austin had gone pale as unbaked dough. He leaned forward in his seat. "Daughter, are you absolutely certain?"

Kayla released the words in one sibilant rush. "I'm sure. It's him."

Honor said, "I don't understand."

Adam hit the Play button. Geoffrey Rambling strode down the sidewalk toward them. Adam had not noticed at the time that Geoffrey had been with others. There were four of them. They all wore their entry badges snaked around their necks. The MVP logo was vividly clear.

Geoffrey was front and center. A woman walked to his left, hard-faced and aggressive, her dark hair chopped short as a man's. Another trader. The other two men were clearly junior in age and rank, for they kept a half pace behind the pair and laughed in sycophantic fashion at everything the traders said.

Honor said, "This is the man who robbed your project? He's here? In London?"

Geoffrey wore a topcoat and a cashmere scarf and a silk tie that glistened in the shadow light. He moved with a predator's grace. He grinned at something the woman trader said.

Adam froze the picture again. There alongside the anger and the pain came the first faint whisper of an idea.

Kayla protested, "That's enough."

"No," Peter said. "I need to know. Are you absolutely certain?"

"Yes."

"Beyond any doubt whatsoever? Because this is—"

Kayla pointed a trembling hand at the screen. "That is Geoffrey Rambling. Now turn it off. Please."

Only when the television went gray did Adam realize he was sweating.

Honor asked, "Will someone please tell me why that man was at that company?"

Peter was much swifter off the mark. "He works there, doesn't he?"

Adam said, "Yes."

"What was his name again?"

"Steen. Derek Steen."

The television might have gone blank. But Geoffrey Rambling still filled the room. The air positively reeked from his invasion.

Peter's breathing rasped harshly in the silent room. "Geoffrey must have been sent down by the group. They knew about our plans to use the project in our new promotion."

"A liar and a thief," Honor said. "A charlatan."

"A psychopath," Kayla said. "I gave him everything. And you see how much it bothers him."

Peter's breath came out in a fluttering sound. "This is how it feels to grow old." His gaze was empty as the television screen. "Faced with another struggle, only this time without the will to fight."

Honor massaged his neck. "You're not old."

"I've been fighting them for sixteen years." He looked at his wife. "Perhaps I should raise the white flag."

Adam said, "No."

The two women looked at him. Kayla's gaze held the quality of light through shattered gemstone. Honor inspected him gravely. Neither spoke.

Peter Austin continued to address his wife. "I could use this, you know. Reveal what we know about this man's actions. Threaten them with a very public revelation. Force them to offer a proper price for my team."

"No," Adam repeated, more forcefully this time. "You just said it yourself. *Your team.* They are *counting* on you."

Honor shepherded them into the dining area, put the kettle on to boil, and fixed a tray for tea. Adam and Kayla were directed to make sandwiches. Adam sawed slices from a whole-grain loaf while Kayla piled on cheese and chutney and mayonnaise and lettuce. Peter sat at the dining table alone, staring out the French doors at a valley draped in winter's gray wreath. Honor planted four clay churns on the table, one each for butter and marmalade and honey and homemade duck pâté. She rolled out dough for biscuits while Adam laid a fire. The fireplace was set so the flames could be seen from the dining room table, and the kitchen area was soon filled with the comforting flavors of cedar smoke and fresh-baked bread.

Honor seated herself at the table's head and said, "Peter, dear."

He came slowly around. "Yes?"

"The blessing."

"You do the honors. I fear my own communications are rather feeble just now."

Adam used the silent meal to review his idea. The longer he worked, the better it felt. There was a high risk factor, even a degree of personal danger. But a strong possible gain. For everyone. When the meal was over, he asked Peter, "Could you give me an overview of your own company's present crisis?"

Peter seemed to have been expecting such a question, for he launched straight in with, "Eleven months ago, we were approached by the British subsidiary of an Italian company. They are Europe's largest specialists in taking new pharmaceuticals and medical equipment through the testing process and bringing them to market. They obtained the rights to partner with the Radcliffe Hospital. Radcliffe is the teaching hospital for Oxford

University's medical school. The Italians announced in utter confidence their subsidiary was ready to be spun off. They offered us the chance to take them to market." Peter broke off a segment of bread and rolled it between his thumb and forefinger. "The deal was extremely favorable."

Adam read the results from the chairman's features. "You overextended your company and the deal went south."

"Not just the company. One proviso that sets us apart from other would-be financial advisers is that we *partner* with our investors. Whatever deal we put forward, we invest our own money."

"You're in too deep personally," Adam said.

"The project proved hopelessly complex. The company directors grew impossible to deal with. Finally we learned why."

"They were hiding financial constraints," Adam said. "Quasi-illegal issues. Bouncing them from the parent to the subsidiary and back again."

Honor asked, "How did you know?"

"It had to be that or something like it," Adam replied. He could see the strain of endless bad news in Peter Austin's features. "They drained off the profits, they switched the patents to a shell company, they stole the good, and they left you holding the bag."

"If we back out," Peter Austin said, "we could be driven into bankruptcy."

"And if you stay," Adam finished for him, "you could be party to an international fraud."

"Our good name is our most important asset."

"Which is why they went after you in this fashion," Adam said.

"Who?" Honor asked. "The Italian company?"

The company chairman replied, "I fear not, my dear."

This time it was Kayla who said, "We have to make them pay."

chapter 20

*W*hen dinner was over, Adam discovered he was staying the night. The invitation was so natural he found no space for refusal, even if he wanted, which he didn't. Honor handed him Peter's largest set of sweat clothes and sent him upstairs. The guestroom was in the alcove over the kitchen. All the family bedrooms were in the newer stone portion of the house, upstairs above Peter's study. The house was silent when Adam came back downstairs from his shower. Adam found Peter seated in the living room, staring blankly at a dying fire. "Thanks for the clothes."

Peter gave him a mildly unfocused look. "They fit all right?"

"Fine."

Peter motioned Adam into the chair next to his. "Has Kayla told you about her mother?"

"A little."

"Look at Kayla and you see Amanda. The intelligence, the drive, the astonishing way she throws herself into her passions." He stared at the fire for a time. "Amanda had lung problems all her life. Phlebitis finally took her. It was a dreadful time for

Kayla. Amanda sent her to boarding school in America, mistakenly thinking it would be best for Kayla not to be around for the worst bits. Other than that, the two of them never fought. None of the standard mother-daughter struggles. They were . . ."

"Friends."

"I was about to say, inseparable. But yes. Friends as well." Peter coughed hard, then rasped, "Then my daughter grows up with all the spirit and passion of her mother. She dedicates her life to this astounding project, only to be brought low by the same vile group that has dogged me for years."

Adam watched Peter struggle from his chair. "Can I ask you something?"

Peter waved a weary hand.

"Why did you hire me? The company is in crisis, you're faced with an impossible situation. Why add something new?"

"Honor asked me the very same thing. I will tell you what I told her, for there is no other answer I can give you." He shuffled wearily across the floor. "I felt the hand of God upon our meeting."

Adam sat in the empty room long after the last light had died.

Adam came fully awake at precisely 5:17. He knew because the only light he could see was an illuminated digital clock. He went straight from deep sleep to full alertness. At first he had no idea why. Then the chair on the opposite side of the guestroom creaked, and he realized he had heard the sound in his sleep.

He jerked upright upon the pallet. "Kayla?"

Her whisper was more shiver than sound. "I had a bad dream."

He did a fan-dance with the blanket, slipping into his trousers. He slipped the sweatshirt over his head and rose barefoot from the pallet. "Let's go make some coffee."

Kayla came limply up from the chair. One hand kept a quilt clutched about her shoulders. When he opened the guestroom door and led her downstairs, it was to a silent house.

Honor ordered her kitchen in the manner of someone used to fumbling through mornings. The coffee fixings were all set together, the cups hung from hooks directly over the machine. A platter on the fridge's bottom shelf held the clay crocks of butter and spreadable cheese and marmalade. Adam laid a fire while the coffee brewed. Kayla let herself be lowered into one of the chairs by the fireplace, as pliant as a quilted doll.

"How do you take your coffee?"

"Milk, no sugar."

He doctored their mugs, cut off the kitchen lights, handed her one painted with a smiling kitty, and drew his own chair closer to hers before settling down. He sipped his mug, and waited.

Kayla asked, "Why did your father leave home?"

"Are you trying to avoid talking about what frightened you?"

"Probably."

"When I asked Mom why he'd left, she said she had only two answers for me. First, that no matter how much it hurt her to be alone just then, all she had to do was look at me to know loving my father had been the right thing to do. And second, God would see us through this." Adam stared at the fire for a long moment, then finished, "I didn't think much of those answers at the time."

Kayla raised her mug and realized it was empty. "Could I have some more, please?"

Adam rose from his chair, poured her another mug, brought it back and set another log on the fire. The wave of sparks colored her face in a different light, and for an instant Adam saw her as she might look in an African dawn. Far from the gray and the cold of an English winter. Out where light was harsh and dawn's only veil was dust and need. He had a sudden impulse to lean over and kiss her. Kayla looked at him, her gaze filled with a submission that defeated him.

He returned to his chair and waited.

"I dreamed about all the mistakes I made with Geoffrey." She brushed a wisp of hair from her forehead. "I woke up feeling powerless to keep from making the same mistakes again. No matter how hard I try. No matter how much I want . . ."

Adam shifted his chair closer and reached for her. She allowed herself to be bundled up, quilt and all, and resettled in his lap. She curled her arms around his neck and rested her head upon his shoulder. Adam smelled the clean sweet scent of her hair, the faint trace of perfume, the heady flavor of her skin. His mind kept repeating two dreadful words. *Four days.*

She said soft as the rising dawn, "I wish I knew what to do."

chapter 21

$\mathcal{T}$he call came after breakfast, while Peter and Honor attended morning service. Kayla listened as Adam took it on his new cell phone. Adam responded with the terse punches of a man receiving news he had been half expecting. Adam finished the call, turned to her, and used the same tone when explaining to her what needed doing. Kayla accepted his plan and went to dress for what would no doubt be an enormously difficult day. Such a submissive nature was not her style. But just then, it was all she could do to accept what she was finding inside herself. She trusted this man.

Adam left Peter and Honor a note. They borrowed Peter's car again and headed for his rooms on Norham Gardens Road. The day was still and not particularly cold. They slipped into Oxford ahead of the worst of the morning rush hour. Kayla waited in the car while Adam went upstairs to change. The sun rose over the buildings opposite and illuminated a silent lane and its canopy of winter-bare trees. Kayla thought briefly about the previous night's dreams and the fears that had driven her from her bed. She sat in the car's rising chill and reflected on how it had been, entering Adam's room and watching him sleep. She had felt so protected there, and yet so vulnerable. She shut her eyes and smelled the morning fire and felt Adam's arms wrap around her, offering a comfort stronger than words.

They took the train to London's Paddington Station and a taxi to Saint Catherine's Docks. During both legs of the journey Adam took a number of phone calls. As they passed Saint Paul's Cathedral and entered the money district, Adam announced, "Detective Foley's managed to arrange things like I hoped."

"Thank you, Adam."

He looked at her. "For what?"

"Right now, mostly for thinking for both of us."

His gaze glowed with dark determination, strong as heat. "We've got the break we need. We've prepared the best we can."

"You have," she corrected.

"You'll be fine."

The docklands redevelopment project had transformed three centuries of harbor sprawl into upscale residential condominiums, wine bars, sports complexes, and the sort of shops that catered to the young, the fast, the City's winners. The driver slid the separating window aside and asked, "What number was it you wanted?"

"Just pull up here, thanks." Adam slid the window closed. "Don't say anything about my working for your father's company."

"You have a plan, don't you?"

"More of an angle. Half-finished. Full of holes. But listen, if I touch you on the arm and offer to help, I want you to trust me and don't say anything more."

"Just let you take over?"

"Yes. Can you do that?"

Kayla had a sudden urge to tell him just how absurd that sounded. To trust herself to the strength and care of another man. Instead she said, "The policewoman and the detective are waiting for us."

Detective Bill Foley stood on a sunlit corner with the woman officer Kayla had last seen at Scotland Yard. Foley said, "The bloke is off to Paris on the three-fifteen Eurostar."

The policewoman declared, "I am officially here on behalf of an inquiry made by your company. That clear?"

"As day."

She asked Foley, "You'll do the paperwork to back me up?"

"Before I leave for my evening tea and knees up," Foley confirmed.

"The situation's not changed since we last met. There is nothing I can do officially. No crime on UK soil, no evidence permissible in court. This may be a total loss. But I couldn't just stand by and do nothing." She asked Foley, "You're certain of your information?"

"As rain on my day off." The detective pointed at the building down the block. "Our bloke is upstairs packing as we speak. Gone for two nights."

"How did you happen upon that information?"

"Our lad is not well liked among the female employees in his division."

Kayla said, "What a surprise."

The sky overhead had taken an iron-hard cast. Christmas bunting stretched across the broad lane leading to the river Thames. The sidewalks were full of couples bundled against the dropping temperatures. Up ahead Kayla could see lights festooned about the pinnacles of Tower Bridge.

Derek Steen lived in a renovated Victorian warehouse. The structure was built like a mock brick fortress whose interior courtyard contained two Porsches and a Bentley. The courtyard was fronted by steel-barred gates.

Foley said, "Our bloke occupies the penthouse."

Kayla looked up. The top floor was rimmed by a waist-high glass wall. Planters held a variety of winter firs. The penthouse had a spectacular view of Tower Bridge and the Thames.

Adam stepped in close and murmured, "He hasn't won yet."

Kayla felt consumed by an emotion she could not name. Which was absurd. If a feeling was so strong it electrified her entire body, she should at least be able to call it something. Yet this was neither fear nor rage. Certainly not eagerness. She dreaded the confrontation, yet could not wait for it to begin and then be done. She fiercely wanted to walk away from this thief.

They stood at the building's bottom step. Officer Walton said, "I suppose this is where I should take the lead."

Adam said, "We can't thank you enough for helping."

"This is why I became a copper. To help the innocent. I knew from the outset I wouldn't right every wrong. That lies in the realm of Providence, and I'm no angel. I'll tell you that up front, and if you don't believe me, you can have a word with my dear old mum. She'll straighten you out right sharpish."

"Protecting the innocent," Adam said. "That's us."

Officer Walton started up the front steps. "Something tells me this is going to be a fine day indeed."

The main entrance was reinforced glass doors in a steel frame. A sentry camera was imbedded in the ceiling. Every other floor had four apartments; the top floor had one. Adam reached for Kayla's arm. She jerked at his touch. Her body had become one great generator. The current just waited for a chance to surge.

Adam said, "You need to step over to one side."

Detective Foley agreed, "If the bloke sees you he'll bolt."

The policewoman pressed the top-floor buzzer. There was a moment's wait, then a male voice said, "You've got the wrong flat."

Kayla's gut knotted so tight she wanted to scream. Adam's hand returned and rested on her arm.

The policewoman replied, "Not if you happen to be Mr. Derek Steen, sir."

"I'm headed out of the country. Come back another time."

"And I am Officer Walton with Scotland Yard. I'd like to have a word."

"Show me your badge."

She unfolded her ID and held it to the camera.

"What's this about?"

"I'd prefer to discuss that in person. May I come up, please?"

The first words out of his mouth were, "I can explain."

Kayla, she of the full-body tremors, responded with the ease of a woman who had spent all night preparing. Instead of not having a proper thought to her name until that very moment.

"That would be a truly astonishing feat," she calmly replied.

His hair was a shade lighter than she recalled. And his face was flabbier, as though the features were gradually melting. Geoffrey looked dissipated. He had it all, and it was eating away at his core.

"I didn't . . ." Then he stopped.

"Should I call you Derek or Geoffrey?"

He looked from Kayla to the cop and back again.

"You're a thief," Kayla said. "Of course I came with the police."

She had dreamed of this moment. Screaming at him. Clawing at him with talons. Shredding him to the bone. Watching him bleed. And beg. And finally reduced to nothing before her eyes.

Now all she felt was ashes.

Geoffrey said, "I want my attorney."

The policewoman replied, "You are certainly welcome to contact whomever you wish, Mr. Steen. But I must inform you that we are not here to arrest you."

Geoffrey tried for a sneer. "Arrest me for what?"

Kayla took a careful look around. In Dar es Salaam, Geoffrey had lived in one of the finest hotels, which was not saying much. The establishment was run by a respectable Indian family. He had paid extra for a larger room with a working AC and daily maid service. He had claimed to have family money.

Kayla did not know what she had expected to find. A glimpse into who this man actually was, perhaps. But the apartment possessed the sterile charm of an expensive hotel suite. The rear windows framed an astonishing view of the river and the bridge and the morning traffic. The interior was carefully coordinated in designer fashion, a muted series of russets and browns, no doubt this year's masculine colors. The place was beautiful, expensive, and heartless. Kayla turned her attention back to the man. The apartment suited him perfectly.

Geoffrey did not snarl. But almost. "What are you smiling at?"

Her own calm was the answer. Kayla said, "It should be obvious, Geoffrey."

"Stop calling me that."

"What would you have me call you then? Thief? Criminal? Fraud? Liar? Phony?"

He gestured irritably. "Call me whatever you want."

Adam touched her arm. "May I?"

Kayla gestured without taking her eyes off the man she did not know. "This is my associate."

Geoffrey re-aimed his sneer. "Going down-market, are we?"

Adam said, "We have a proposition for you."

He reached for his telephone. "I'm phoning my solicitor."

Adam was ready for that. "Ask him to meet us at MVP headquarters."

"What?"

"No doubt it's hard to make an appointment with your chairman. But I would imagine Rupert Madden could find time for Scotland Yard."

Blotchy spots appeared as he slipped the phone into his back pocket. "You don't think Madden knows?"

"Oh, he might *surmise*. No doubt he *assumed* something like this happened. But if the press were to catch wind of this, which they will, will he stand up for you?"

For the first time, Kayla thought of him as Derek. She shaped the name in her mind and applied it to this stranger standing before her. Derek Steen was afraid. Of Adam.

Derek said, "That's slander."

The policewoman said, "Actually, sir, slander only occurs when the rumors are untrue."

Adam said, "We'd be delighted to see this situation played out in the court of public opinion. What do you think would happen to your career, Derek?"

"What do you want?"

"Two things. First, what do you know about MVP's role in bringing down Austin's firm?"

Derek blanched whiter still. "Nothing. That is . . . There isn't any such plan."

"Your future depends upon honesty here, Derek."

"I don't know anything about this. It's total fabrication."

"We're not after prosecuting you, Derek. We're after saving Oxford Ventures."

"There's not . . . I am not aware of anything of that nature."

Adam gave it a moment, the silence dragging tight as the air grating in Derek's throat. Then, "You owe Kayla some funds. How much was it again?"

"Six hundred thousand pounds," Kayla said. "And my watch."

"I never . . ."

Officer Walton said, "I have checked the records this morning, sir. I must inform you that Britain has very clear agreements with Tanzania governing the extradition of felons."

"But we don't want that," Adam said. "Not any more than we want to bring the press into your chairman's office."

Adam glanced at her. Kayla knew what was required. "You *robbed* me. You owe me."

Derek's gaze slipped back and forth like a frantic eel. "I don't have anything like that amount."

Adam asked, "Where's your checkbook, Derek?"

His gaze slipped to where his briefcase lay open on the dining room table. Instantly he drew it back. Too late.

Adam walked over and searched among the papers. He extracted a slender kidskin case and a silver pen. He walked back and set both on the side table by Derek's hand. "We have a special going. This morning only. You're going to write out a check for half of what you stole."

"I can't—"

Officer Walton said, "Far be it from me to advise a member of the public on such a matter, Mr. Steen. But I understand the prisons in Dar es Salaam are quite inadequate."

"We're not going there, though, are we?" Adam said. "Just

like we're not interested in taking a meeting with Madden. And calling the press."

"You're mad, the lot of you. Nobody has that sort of cash laying about."

"That's a real shame, Derek." He walked around the counter and hefted the phone. "Who do we call first, your chairman or your attorney?"

Derek's gaze dropped to the checkbook. "I could possibly manage half that."

"Write out the check to Kayla Austin," Adam said. "Then call your bank and do whatever you need to make sure the funds are waiting for us. Do that, and all this goes away. We walk out of your life."

Adam looked at her. And nodded once. Kayla felt the electric current pass between them, stronger than words. She supplied, "Just like you walked out of mine."

chapter 22

*A*dam took care of everything. He thanked the security agent and the policewoman for them both. He flagged a taxi and went to the nearest branch of Derek's bank. He coached Kayla through signing the check and requesting a banker's check made out to cash. They then traveled to the brokerage agency where he had set up her account. Kayla sat and let their investment discussions wash over her.

Adam took her back to the taxi and said, "There's one more thing I need to take care of before we go."

"Can it wait?"

"I know you're exhausted. But this has to happen now."

Adam asked the taxi to find them an inexpensive hotel near Paddington Station. The driver pulled up in front of a Victorian row house whose rooms were large and slightly seedy. Entering the room he had secured, Adam pulled the frayed cover off the bed and watched Kayla sink onto the mattress. "A hundred and fifty thousand pounds was as far as I thought I could push him."

Kayla realized he took her silence as regret, or disappointment, and was apologizing. "We needed this so much."

"I wish it was more."

The words did not come easily, for to shape them meant giving structure to hope. She had lived so long without any. "We might be able to turn everything around now."

"That's my thinking. At least you've got more time to try." He checked his watch. "I need to go out for a while. I'll be back as soon as I can."

"All right." The last thing she heard was the door opening and closing. Kayla dove into sleep.

She drifted back toward the surface several times. Once when the door opened, and she opened her eyes long enough to see it was Adam. Again when the room became tainted by some sharp chemical smell. Kayla sat up and swung her feet to the floor and rubbed her face. "Adam?"

The bathroom door cracked open. Light spilled into the darkened room. "I'm here."

She rubbed her face again. "How long have I been asleep?"

"A couple of hours. Maybe a little longer." Adam pushed open the door.

Kayla rose to her feet and backed until she met the wall. Derek Steen entered the room. But it was Adam who said, "It's me."

He walked over and turned on the switch by the door. Kayla felt the world return to gradual focus. Adam wore Derek like a suit. "I took Derek's company pass from his briefcase when I fetched his checkbook."

"You're going inside MVP?"

"We need to see if Derek has anything to help your dad, Kayla."

"That's crazy!"

"Listen to me." Adam's calm was unnerving. "Getting the money for your project was only half the battle."

All her possible responses created a jumbled mess in her brain, such that the only one to emerge was, "Joshua fired you!"

Adam pointed at the table by the window. "I've brought you a sandwich and a juice."

"I'm not hungry."

"You need to eat, Kayla."

She made it around the bed and over to the window without taking her eyes off him. As she passed the bathroom, she smelled the odor again and realized, "You've dyed your hair."

He followed her over but did not sit down beside her. The room had an old-fashioned bay window with heavy green drapes. Outside there was the rumble and hiss of city traffic. "I need to look enough like him that anybody I pass won't be alarmed."

She peeled away the sandwich cover and took a bite. "You went out and bought his clothes."

"Close as I could find."

"It's amazing."

Adam wore a copy of Derek's clothes from that morning. They formed a version of city casual—cashmere sweater over a pin-striped shirt with a white collar, and a flashy foulard knotted about his neck. Fawn-colored gabardine slacks. Italian loafers. Gold watch that dangled loose.

She leaned more closely. "Are you wearing contacts?"

"Eye color was something I couldn't risk having wrong."

"And your face. How did you . . ."

"Makeup." His features possessed a hint of Derek's slackness. The tinted hair was slicked back and spiked. His eyes were gray now, not quite as light as Derek's, but enough for someone who merely glanced his way. "These are tricks, Kayla. Like cue cards."

Adam stood by the window drapes and watched her eat. Several times he started to speak, then caught himself. Kayla waited until she finished the sandwich and drank the last of the orange juice to ask, "What is it?"

"When we were away over the weekend, you said how perfect it was for me to escape into acting roles. Well, you were right. On the show, my role was the dissipated playboy, the guy who could have any woman and usually did. In a lot of the episodes, I needed to go from the night before to the day after. But there's more."

When he did not continue, Kayla said softly, "More."

"A good actor has to find some core identification with the character and the role. When I met Derek, I saw myself."

"You're not him."

"Not who I am. Who I almost became." He lifted one edge of the drapes and stared at the night. "I was so close."

Just after eleven, Adam paid his taxi and climbed the stairs leading from the street to the MVP headquarters. The big chrome-and-glass doors swung open before him. Adam stepped inside and crossed the lobby. He hid his dread behind a Derek-style frown. Or so he hoped. The guard behind the curved reception desk watched him but did not rise from his seat. Adam pulled his cell phone from one pocket and the pass he had palmed from Derek's briefcase in the other. He pretended to pay attention to the phone while he approached the steel barrier. He slid the pass through the magnetic barrier and then leaned into the revolving bars. They clicked around, granting him entry.

He faced three banks of elevators. He punched the hotel number and stood in pretended concentration while he searched for the bank of elevators that serviced the seventh floor. When the hotel answered, he asked to be put through to Kayla's room, and then headed for the central bank.

"Adam?"

"I'm in."

She breathed easier for both of them. "You have the detective's instructions?"

"Right here." Detective Foley and his in-house source had come through for them again. Adam touched the pocket containing the notes from his telephone conversation, detailing the layout of Derek Steen's floor. But Adam doubted he would need them. They were there for assurance's sake. Like the words of dialogue he used to write on the inside of his palm, to trigger his memory in case of a panic attack. Adam stepped into the elevator, punched the button for seven, and tried to convince himself that it was just another role.

"Be careful," Kayla said. "And come out of this safely."

"Do my best."

"I mean it. That's the most important thing tonight. Your safety. Daddy would agree a hundred percent."

"This is one gig we don't need to be telling the old man about, though, do we?" The double doors fronting the elevators were red leather embossed with the MVP logo. Adam ran the pass through another magnetic reader, and the doors swept open to reveal the currency trading floor. He started down the central aisle.

"Where are you?"

"The money pit."

"Where?"

The currency floor occupied almost the entire seventh floor. The windowless chamber was a hundred feet square with a thirty-foot-high ceiling. A supervisor's balcony overlooked one end and running electronic newsboards the other. The desks were split into a dozen islands crammed inside a sea of green carpet. A cluster of late-working peons shuffled papers on a long table by the far wall. The odor of empty pizza cartons wafted across the room. "Once I thought there would be nothing finer than working here."

"I thought you were escaping to Costa Rica."

"Costa one week, a trading pit the next. Become the super analyst, held in awe by the traders who fought to sign my checks. Power in both fists. Money to burn."

Each island, or trading station, had between six and fourteen desks. The senior trader occupied the central position. Some of the largest islands had two traders, but not many. Geoffrey's station was in the far northeast corner. Each seat had a triple set of screens, except the senior, which held a double-stack so he could monitor his own positions and check on any of his juniors at the same time.

Kayla said, "Somehow I can't see you happy living that life."

Adam pushed through the glass door at the chamber's far end. "Derek's is the third office on the left?"

"According to the detective's notes."

Only the senior traders had offices. Adam had been around enough trading floors to know they were not expected to spend much time there. The office and the window were perks. Derek's was not large. Nor did it appear much·lived-in. Adam slipped into Derek's leather throne. The window overlooked an empty London street. A single photo adorned the opposite wall, Derek behind the oversize wheel of an oceangoing yacht. A pair of Ray-Bans dangled around his neck. Flashing his pirate's smile. Cold. Aloof. Invulnerable. Alone.

"Adam?"

"I'm turning on his computer."

"Can anyone see you?"

"The door is glass, but the hallway is empty." He fought off a sudden sensation of the chair imprisoning him, as though the real owner's ire was able to reach out and gnaw at his bones. "Okay, it's asking for a password."

Kayla's voice grew a metallic rasp. "Back in Dar es Salaam he kept a slip of paper in the bottom of his top right drawer. He could never remember when I changed the project codes."

"Okay. It's here." He read the seven digits off the paper, typed them in, slipped the paper back in the drawer and slid it shut. "Uh-oh."

"What's the matter?"

"I'm looking at a second check-in screen. He's set in *another* password."

"He's got something to hide."

"Maybe so."

"No maybe, Adam. He's in this up to his eyeballs."

"What difference does that make, if we can't get in?" Frantically he searched the other drawers, then felt around the base of the desk. "Nothing."

"Tell me what you see."

"The screen shows a picture of him on a racetrack. He's standing beside a Ferrari Formula One car." The photo also showed Derek's arms wrapped around two beauties wearing Ferrari T-shirts and red-leather hot pants. Adam saw no need to mention that to Kayla. "There's a box in the middle of the screen asking for another password."

"Which means this is his own backup system and not standard company operations."

"Probably." Adam wiped his face. "This is taking too long."

Kayla went quiet. Then, "Try my name."

Adam hesitated a long moment, then typed in the name. He paused with his hand over the Enter tab. Then pressed it.

And breathed a long sigh. "We're in."

chapter 23

*T*hey did not make it back to the Austin residence until after two in the morning. Derek Steen's computer files had proven infuriatingly bare of usable evidence. Adam ran a search covering various names—Peter's company, Oxford University, the hospital doing clinical trials, the Italian company. Brief snippets appeared here and there, terse fragments that could well have been some company code. Given weeks, Adam suspected he could have come up with a clear trail of misdeeds. But Adam did not have weeks. Each passing minute brought an increased risk of discovery. Finally Adam did a wholesale dump of Steen's entire filing system and zipped it off to his own e-mail address. And fled.

Despite the shortened night, Adam awoke not just clear-headed, but with a precise knowledge of his next step. A lifetime's worth of arguments meant nothing in the face of this certainty. When Honor and Peter entered the kitchen below his bedroom, he dressed and went downstairs to join them. But he had no intention of sharing with them the fragments and guesses that had been gained from his search. And the confrontation with Derek was Kayla's story to relate. Instead, he took his mug over to the rear doors and savored dawn's slow arrival. Circling hawklike in the growing light was a whisper from his past. His twelfth birthday had fallen on a Sunday. Adam had celebrated by asking his mother not to make him go to church again. Not then, not ever. Even at twelve, Adam had been determined to go places, and do so on his own terms. He was going to be strong. He was going to *win*.

Instead of all the arguments he had spent weeks steeling himself against, his mother had simply replied, "One day I hope you come to understand the difference between religion and faith, between the church and the body of Christ."

Adam saw both the mist-clad valley and his own hollow-eyed reflection. All this time, and he still had no idea what she had been talking about.

Well, it was time he started finding out.

When he turned around, Honor asked, "Have you colored your hair?"

"Yes. It's a long story."

Peter's rasp had deepened to where he scarcely had any voice at all. "It's time we left for church."

Adam set his mug on the counter and said what had been waiting for him when he awoke. "Could I come with you?"

Honor asked, "To the morning service?"

"If it's all right."

"Of course it's all right. We'd be delighted to have you join us, wouldn't we, Peter?"

But as Peter opened his mouth to respond, a soft voice asked, "Can I come too?"

Tendrils of mist glowed yellow in the lights surrounding the church. The bell sounded muffled, a tolling soft as the pre-dawn. Villagers offered one another quiet greetings as they passed through the perimeter walls. Footsteps scrunched across the graveled forecourt. The bell tolled a final time as they climbed the front steps, the sound lingering long in the chill and the damp.

The church's interior was far narrower than the outer structure suggested. A placard by the entrance said the edifice dated from 1087 and was built upon the foundations of a far older church, one that had never been successfully dated, though records from the eighth century mentioned a monastery on the site. Kayla followed her father and Honor down the central aisle. Candles flanked the aisle and the front altar. Honor slipped into a pew close to the front. The church was neither full nor empty. Kayla guessed their numbers at about fifty.

A woman muffled against the wintry chill rose from the first pew and approached the dais. The ritual returned to Kayla with the soft familiarity of an old and dear friend. She murmured words she had once taken pride in forgetting. Her mind flitted to the service, to Peter on one side of her, and Honor on the other, and Adam on her father's other side. Kayla observed how Adam studied the missal with such intensity the air seemed to shimmer about him.

Her long nap in the seedy London hotel had left her unable to sleep once they finally returned home. Instead, she had tossed and turned through the dark hours, chased from sleep by two thoughts. No, she corrected, *thought* was not a strong enough term. They were certainties. She knew with absolute conviction that they were both true; first, that Adam loved her, and second, that she did not have it within herself to give what he needed.

But what finally drove her from her bed was the question asked in a predawn hush, yet resounding through her with explosive force.

Did she *want* to give to him, to answer his needs, to love and be loved?

If so, she had no choice. She could never find what was required inside herself. Not if she searched the ashes of her poor charred heart for a hundred lifetimes. Trust and confidence and hope and love. All the words she had cast aside as belonging to a different person, a different era, a different life. If she wanted to give to him what he needed, what he *deserved*, she had to look elsewhere.

They rose to their feet a second time, all but Adam. It was unlikely he realized the others had moved at all, his concentration was so complete.

The church was built in the medieval fashion, with walls almost six feet thick at the base, narrowing in pyramidal fashion as they rose to the high ceiling. The narrow stained-glass windows were a pale wintry wash. The candlelight formed a comforting haven where even the flickering shadows were friendly.

Kayla shut her eyes and felt her mother's presence so intensely she had to resist the urge to reach over and grip the hand that was not there. She took a shaky breath, and her nostrils were filled with her mother's favorite perfume. Somehow her mother had bridged the eternal divide, just so she could share in this moment. Kayla found the presence so powerful, so comforting, the questions and the doubt and the pain just washed away. A calm replaced it all, the ashes and the hurt and the scorn and the fractured dreams, a calm so potent she could not entirely hold back the tears.

She opened her eyes and stood for the final blessing. The church swam in a gentle glow of candlelight and remembrances so strong they did not vanish merely because the moment was over. Kayla wiped her face and wondered if what she had just experienced might be called a prayer.

chapter 24

*P*eter, Honor, and Kayla left the church ahead of Adam. Their footsteps scrunched across the graveled forecourt. They walked with their heads close together. Peter coughed, and both women reached over to touch his back. A family.

They piled coats and mittens and scarves on the same chair, then filed down the central passage and through the living room and into the kitchen. Adam helped the two ladies set the table and put on a fresh pot of coffee and slice bread and lay out fruit and cheese and marmalade. He was grateful for the silence. For Adam it felt as though words would have cluttered a morning that had already moved far beyond speech and normal comprehension.

Honor brewed Peter a mug of tea, then laced it with honey and fresh ginger. "Let's see if this eases your throat."

Peter blew, sipped, sighed, sipped again. Then he rasped, "Thank you both for coming this morning. It means more than I can possibly say."

Honor took her seat beside her husband. "I think you should ask him, dear."

"Do you?"

"It seems to me the morning has given you the only answer you require." Honor turned to Adam and went on, "Peter has a daunting task ahead of him today."

"A luncheon," Peter said.

"A trial," Honor corrected. "Peter fears the verdict is a foregone conclusion."

"We must keep hold of hope," Peter murmured.

Honor's worried gaze remained on Peter as she continued, "Some of Peter's largest investors will be there."

"Bursars of two colleges." It clearly pained him to speak. "Representatives of three other endowments. The chief accountant of the university's science faculty. And one of the university library directors."

Honor finished, "And Rupert Madden. You know who he is?"

"CEO of Madden and Van Pater," Adam said, and resisted the urge to talk about their foray into MVP headquarters. It would only add to the day's burdens.

Honor went on, "We were wondering, that is, Peter was hoping perhaps you might help him prepare."

Adam set down his cup. "That's why I'm here."

Adam spent a grueling two hours helping Peter as much as was possible. The facts were arranged. The argument made as precise as possible. By the time they finished, Peter's voice had been reduced to a scant whisper.

When Peter went upstairs to dress, Honor and Kayla joined Adam in the kitchen. Honor asked, "What do you think?"

Adam replied carefully, "I understand your concerns."

Kayla said, "I wish you could have known Daddy before all this. This past year has aged him a decade."

"Peter has always balanced his business drive and acumen with a genuine compassion," Honor said. "So remarkable for a man holding that kind of corporate power."

"A real gentleman," Kayla said.

"Confident, yet willing to hear others out and change his mind."

"Strong and kind at the same time," Kayla said.

"People become so devoted to him." Honor wiped one cheek. "And he feels the same way. Which is why these events have taken such a terrible toll. I honestly believe he worries more over the employees Joshua has dismissed than his company."

Kayla bit her lip. "He's the strongest man I've ever known."

Peter's tread down the stairs turned Honor around. "And the finest."

Kayla said, "I wish we could find a way to bring him back."

As Adam drove them into town, Peter Austin sat with his briefcase open in his lap, leafing through the pages of his speech. Adam had gone through the material so often he could have recited it by heart, but he doubted Peter even noticed what he held. The man's gaze was hollowed by what he feared had already happened. The car remained silent until Adam pulled onto Norham Gardens Road and said, "I'll change as fast as I can."

Peter studied the redbrick house. "This is Sylvia's home?"

"Professor Beachley. Yes."

"I haven't seen her since Amanda's funeral." He glanced over, uncertain. "Should I go in?"

Adam opened his door. "It would absolutely make her day."

The idea came to him as he was knotting his tie. It arrived not with a thunderbolt, but a whisper. He checked his complexion and felt the difference immediately. No longer the young protégé helping his ailing boss. Now he was an actor preparing for the spotlight. If only Peter granted him the chance to play the role.

When he entered the downstairs parlor, Professor Beachley smiled her approval. "Aren't you the dashing young man."

Peter was seated in the other horsehair armchair. The parlor's lighting turned his features cavernous. "Given time, Adam could become my strong right arm."

"I hope you'll forgive me for saying so, Peter, dear. But you need one. You appear on the brink of collapse."

"We are facing a rather serious struggle."

"Adam and your daughter told me a bit about your current situation." Her smile returned. "What a delight it was to see Kayla again. She has grown into the mirror image of your dear Amanda. The two of them have proven a veritable tonic."

"For me as well." Peter turned to Adam. "Shall we be off?"

"Not just yet." Adam took a deep breath and launched straight in. "I want you to let me give the speech today."

"My dear young man—"

"You're worn out. You've said it yourself. I've watched you fumble your lines all morning. I know what you want to say. They'll see your state as clearly as we do and understand why I'm the one who speaks."

The professor murmured, "Oh, I say. What a brilliant concept."

"I couldn't possibly . . ." The chairman's gaze shifted back and forth between them. "Joshua just fired you."

Adam had no response to that except, "I can do this, Peter."

The professor leaned forward. "Peter, dear, I want you to pay careful attention to what I'm about to tell you. You must do what he says. Do you hear me? I feel God's hand upon this young man and his offer."

Adam did not give his boss another chance to object. He rose from his chair and said, "We've got to be going."

"Adam, dear, write out a number where I can reach you."

"No problem." He slipped a pad and pen from his coat pocket. "This is my cell phone."

"Thank you. As you may recall, there is an issue with one of my former students. Hearing you speak just now has left me even more certain that you are the solution to her crisis." She reached over and patted Adam's hand. "Just as you are to Peter's."

The medieval faculties of Oxford University stood at the heart of the city. The street was jammed and exuberant and cold. An iron-hard wind pressed relentlessly among the students and tourists. They passed the Radcliffe Camera, the rotund arena where university convocations were held in gilt and grandeur, and entered a paved courtyard through towering gates. The surrounding portals bore gold-leaf inscriptions from another era: *Schola Logicae, Schola Astronomiae et Rhetoricae, Schola Musicae, Schola Naturalis Philosophiae, Schola Medicinae*. Oxford's original Divinity School stood at the center. Time-stained windows observed a quad of singular charm and unaffected elegance. Scholars strolled the stone courtyard or sat muffled against the cold.

The old Divinity School was shaped like a medieval chapel. The main hall was a severe place, walled in ornately carved stone and crowned by gilded beams thick as Adam's chest. The flagstone floor undulated from the currents of time. A long table occupied the chamber's center, formally laid in crystal and damask. The narrow windows were adorned with stained-glass collegiate crests.

Adam observed all this from the broad vestibule. He stood partially hidden behind the coatracks and observed the chairman of MVP approach Peter. There was no mistaking Rupert Madden. He moved with a lion's elegant force. The entire gathering paused and watched the princes from opposing courts, whose handshake was a formality that disguised nothing.

Madden's greeting rang with smug triumph. "Ah, Peter. I wondered whether you'd actually show up today."

"Rupert."

"I suppose I should offer condolences of one form or another."

Peter tried to stifle his cough and failed. "For what?"

Madden exuded a cold, implacable force. He was a man who relished applying the dagger, who could kill dreams with abandon and take pleasure in ruined hopes. "Why, the demise of your little firm, of course."

"You always were overly swift in your assumptions."

Rupert Madden turned away. "Not this time."

Adam had seen enough. Never had Peter Austin's core qualities stood in clearer contrast to the world Adam had long chased after. Peter was not merely deeper or more considerate or more caring than his opponent. Despite his flushed features and evident illness, there was no question in Adam's mind who was truly the stronger man.

Adam slipped the pad and pen from his pocket and wrote a swift note. He tore off the page, then counted the bills in his wallet. He folded half his money and took a moment to study the passing waiters. The one he selected had a hard look about him, with a shaved head and shoulders that stretched his white jacket tight as a drumhead. "Can I have a moment?"

"We're busy here, mate." But he followed Adam back to the vestibule's outer wall.

"Here's sixty pounds." Adam handed over the money. "It's half of everything I have on me."

The waiter pocketed the folded bills. "You've got a right way of snagging a bloke's attention."

"See the man in the gray suit at the head of the table? The instant he stands up to deliver his speech, I want you to walk over and deliver this note."

The waiter put his tray down on a window ledge. "Walk up and hand him this bit of paper."

"Tell him it's urgent. That he needs to read it immediately."

"No worries."

But Adam stopped him from picking up his tray. "Remember, the moment he gets to his feet. That's vital. Do it and you'll get another sixty pounds when the meeting's over."

When the master called the gathering to order, Adam entered the chamber and took his seat beside Peter. The master gave his opening remarks from his place at the head of the table. Rupert Madden sat to his right, Peter to his left. As the waiters brought in the first course, Peter leaned toward Adam and said, "If Madden succeeds in taking these investors from us, all is lost."

"We can't let that happen." Adam paused while the waiter deposited his plate, then said, "I need you to trust me."

Peter studied Adam intently. "Precisely what do you have in mind?"

"I'm going to shake Madden's tree. Hard. And publicly. Using his own foul deeds."

Peter Austin had the look of a Greek king waiting to fall on his sword. "Nothing breaches Madden's ramparts."

Adam said, "There's a first time for everything."

When the master introduced Rupert Madden, the head of MVP rose to his feet and walked around the head of the table. Peter Austin was forced to either twist around to view his adversary or stare at his plate, lonely and brooding. Madden began, "For two years in a row, Madden and Van Pater has led the UK's mutual fund index." Rupert Madden tapped the back of Adam's chair in proud emphasis to his words. "In today's uncertain markets, with so many fine firms facing confusion and chaos, there is no better company with which to invest your endowments and thus ensure your financial futures."

Adam glanced toward the empty portal, willing the waiter to appear.

"A million pounds invested with Madden and Van Pater two years ago would have netted . . ."

The waiter entered through the rear doors. He walked straight up to Rupert Madden and spoke loud enough for the entire hall to hear. "I'm very sorry to interrupt, sir." He handed over Adam's note. "I'm told this is most urgent."

Madden unfolded the note. His ruddy complexion turned the color of old bones.

Adam's note was brief in the extreme. *Oxford Ventures knows about Derek Steen, Geoffrey Rambling, and Dar es Salaam.*

The Bodleian Library's director asked, "Is everything all right, Mr. Madden?"

Rupert Madden stared at the empty doors, through which the waiter had now vanished.

"Mr. Madden?"

The MVP chairman read the note a second time, looked at Peter Austin in what could only be described as panic, and stuffed the paper into his pocket.

The second sentence of Adam's note was based upon one specific item he had found in the previous night's search. Adam had found no hard evidence. But one word had appeared repeatedly in Steen's computer files. A word that held no possible business meaning, for it named a region of Tanzania that held no industry or commerce whatsoever. Adam knew that for a fact because he had checked. The word was so alien, and used so repeatedly, Adam had been fairly certain it was a code. Seeing the chairman's trembling response, Adam was certain it was a code for something very wrong.

The note's second sentence read, *They know about Serengeti.*

Rupert Madden fumbled through the remainder of his remarks in record time. The Bodleian master watched in bemusement as the MVP chairman found his way back into his seat.

The master said, "Mr. Austin, perhaps you would care to respond?"

Adam rose to his feet, patted Peter on the shoulder, and began, "My chairman is unfortunately not well, and so has asked me to speak on his behalf."

"And you are?"

"Adam Wright."

Peter cleared his throat. "Adam is my protégé."

Adam began, "As some of you know, both Peter and his late wife were students at Christ Church. Last night Peter told me that he had felt her presence very strongly these past few days. Amanda Austin was apparently a great one for the promotion of legacy. And that is what I would like to speak with you about today. The vital importance of building a proper legacy."

Adam's adrenaline surge was such that he could be both intensely involved in his talk and observe himself from a distance. He realized that he had slipped into a role. He was not merely mouthing Peter's speech. He was speaking with the chairman's quiet intensity. And confidence. And ease. Adam strode to the front of the room and reflected that there was nothing more he could wish for himself than to become a man reformed in Peter Austin's mold.

"Before that, however, I am obliged to respond directly to Mr. Madden's comments. There are two points he failed to mention, both of which are of crucial importance. The first, I am sorry to say, is that over the past three quarters our company has lost fourteen percent of its value. As have your holdings. This is the first period in our history that we have not made a profit. Up to last spring, through all the trials and turmoil we have faced together, we have produced a steady return. Which brings us to the second point, which is that over the sixteen years of our existence, capital invested in Oxford Ventures has increased in value by four hundred and eighteen percent. This is fourteen percent more than the same capital would have earned with MVP."

The words came far easier than any scene he had spent

weeks rehearsing. Adam saw with piercing clarity what it meant to portray such a man, and to do so from the inside out. To be a man who cared deeply for his company and his employees and his investors. A man of compassion. A man of vision. A leader. "Certainly the past year's difference in our respective performances is by far the most dramatic of this entire period. There is nothing whatsoever we can say about our disastrous results except that we are sorry. Deeply, deeply sorry. We have let you down."

Adam punctuated an end to that thought by walking around the headmaster's chair. But his destination was not his adversary's seat. Instead, he walked to the far corner of the chamber. He stood over a massive blackened chest, one he had never seen before. But it looked precisely as Peter had described it the previous evening. Adam raised his voice so that it echoed through the stone chamber. "This, as most of you know, is the chest of Sir Thomas Bodley. Safekeeping of money and valuables posed obvious problems in the days before bank vaults and strong rooms. The answer was the medieval treasure chest, which was not protected by locks so much as by weight. This particular chest is banded by both iron and plastered stone. It weighs almost four tons. The result is a chest so heavy thieves could not lift it. The top is fastened by interconnected locking mechanisms and requires four keys to be turned in careful tandem, making it the forerunner of a modern safe's numerical dial.

"In the late thirteen hundreds, Bodley left his money chest and all it contained to this august body. His bequest financed the Bodleian Library, which remains the foremost university library in the world."

Adam left the chest and returned to the table. He rested one hand upon the peak of the master's chair and continued, "Less well known is the history of the chair now occupied by our host. This, my honored colleagues, is the Drake Chair, made from timbers taken from the forecastle of the *Golden Hind*. Which, as you are no doubt aware, is the ship Drake used to circumnavigate the globe. It stands as a silent reminder that Oxford University's geography department became the first to accurately map the globe."

His hand rose and fell once upon the chair. "I ask you to give careful consideration to the concept of legacy. The pressure and pace of this modern era leave us little room to consider what will happen when we are gone. Yet the hall where we are gathered is testimony to that simple fact. We come, we serve, and we depart.

"What is our legacy? Profit or something greater? What gift do we bestow upon those who will follow? Whom, by our actions, do we serve? What is our ultimate purpose?"

Adam returned to stand behind his seat. "Peter Austin did not establish Oxford Ventures merely to compete in the arena of profit. Yes, of course, we have a responsibility to generate revenue. But our *purpose* was to create a legacy. How? By aiding the Oxford community in bringing new ideas to the market. By helping to transform theory into commercial reality. We established a second division which fosters and aids and promotes the local scientific community. Why? Certainly not merely for profit. Many of these ventures will not show a profit for years, perhaps decades, and some never. Oxford Ventures holds to this perilous course because there *is* something greater than profit alone. Because we *do* serve a higher purpose. Because our vision must be focused *beyond* the human horizon."

He paused there for quiet emphasis, then concluded, "Legacy. A vital concept. One we must instill in those around us, those entrusted to our care, the only way we can. By example."

s soon as Adam left with Peter for the meeting in town, Honor sat down at the kitchen table and cupped her face in both hands. All the fear and worry and sleepless distress she had hidden from her husband came out in that single gesture. Kayla walked over and put her arm around her. Such a simple action. One friend being there for another. She did not say anything, just let Honor know she was not alone.

Eventually Honor lifted her elbows off the kitchen table and swept the hair from her face. "I was going to the Christmas market today. I wanted to surprise Peter with a tree and a wreath for the door. But just now I don't feel up to doing anything."

"I'll go. I'd like to."

Honor studied her. "Must you truly leave so soon again for Africa?"

"Yes. My number two, his name is Tanyo. He's Tanzanian. Never been outside his country. He is immensely trustworthy. But he isn't able to handle the project on his own."

"I remember your father saying once that a good assistant does not necessarily make a good leader."

"That's Tanyo in a nutshell."

Honor smiled at the memory. "He was talking about you at the time. Describing why he had never pressured you to join his firm."

"I would have been miserable."

"I understand that now. But understanding doesn't make it any easier for your father, having you so far away."

"I won't make it so long between trips. Not ever again. I promise."

Kayla watched the woman's beautiful features melt slightly. Then recover with sheer internal determination. "I pretend to sleep at night. Knowing I'm awake will only add to his concerns. But I know he's not resting well. He is so worried about me. The house, the firm, the baby, everything all bundled together."

Kayla said, "I want to give Daddy back his money."

"Thank you, sweetheart. That is so incredibly kind. But Peter wouldn't dream of accepting—"

"Adam managed to get back a hundred and fifty thousand pounds. From Geoffrey. I mean, Derek. We didn't talk about it last night, there was so much ground to cover about Daddy's company and MVP. But I have it. And I can give Daddy back his funds."

Honor stared at her a long moment. "Peter would never accept."

Kayla started to argue, but Honor's fragile state defeated her. She would bring it up with Peter.

Honor said, "I'm so glad Adam went with Peter today. And to have you join us at church this morning. You don't know, you can't imagine, how much that meant. Especially today." She hesitated, then asked, "Would you mind terribly if we prayed?"

Kayla neither spoke nor shut her eyes. But she allowed Honor to take hold of both her hands, then sat there and listened to the soft words wash over her. Honor tightened her grip in regular pulses of tension, of confession, of fear. Even so, Kayla felt nothing save a remarkable sense of peace. The calm from that moment, and the way they had embraced at the front door, two friends sharing a very difficult time, stayed with Kayla as she drove into town.

The Christmas market stretched the entire length of Broad Street, nestled among the colleges and their walls of honeyed stone. Sunlight and ruddy faces and good cheer and a fierce winter wind filled the market. Kayla bought a tree so large she could only fit it into Honor's car by bending it slightly. She went back for a holly wreath, and on a sudden impulse purchased a second. The air was laden with chatter and cloves and cinnamon and fresh-baked tarts. Kayla walked until the cold worked its way through her clothing layers and into her bones. There was no reason for how she felt, so light it seemed as though only the holly wreaths kept her from floating away.

When Kayla pulled up in front of the house on Norham Gardens Road, the word that best described the way she felt about stopping by was *natural*.

Professor Beachley greeted her with a delighted, "Oh, my

dear Kayla, what a lovely wreath. Set it there in the hall and come sit down." The old lady beamed as Kayla settled into the seat beside her. "I had the most marvelous chat with your father this morning."

"Daddy stopped by?"

"We spoke while your young man changed clothes. I had quite forgotten what a distinguished gentleman your father is. Despite his rather frail state, he remains so very handsome. I haven't seen Peter since the funeral. He apologized repeatedly for not making it by since. Which was quite unnecessary." She patted Kayla's hand. "I must say, your own young man is quite the looker."

"Adam was an actor. On television."

"Well, I'm hardly surprised. The both of you harbor an air of refined beauty tempered by rather large measures of the world. Not in a bad way, mind. You have been tested by fires which lie far beyond the border of my ivory-towered realm."

Kayla found it the most natural thing in the world to tell her what she faced. Just launch in and share the story. Of her growing feelings for Adam.

When Kayla lapsed into silence, the professor asked, "What do you suppose might be the true purpose behind Oxford's tutorial system?"

Kayla responded with the first thing that came to mind. "To get under the student's skin."

Sylvia Beachley laughed, and her face shed a dozen years. "You are closer to the truth than you might suppose. The task is to *illuminate*. A student comes with a problem, a hope, a pain, a quest. More often than not, students are so tightly enmeshed in their issue, they fail to see vital elements clearly. Which brings us to the matter at hand. Might I have a go at reinterpreting this issue of yours?"

Kayla took a firm grip on the chair's arms. "All right."

"You are at an impasse. Your dreams and ambitions and passions have been reduced to rubble. You have been made an outcast from hope. Your journey home from Africa was driven by desperation. And what happens, but *another* man appears. A wounded hero with his own burdens. One who accepts your quest as his own, who moves heaven and earth to aid you. Suddenly you find yourself within a swirling vortex of new questions and unexpected challenges, which you feel utterly unable to confront. Even your need to return swiftly to salvage what you can of your project is under challenge."

Kayla said, "I have to go back to Dar es Salaam."

"Fine. That is established. You shall go. And soon."

Kayla blinked. She knew there was more. She *craved* it.

"But there is also a new choice which you must make. And here, I feel, is where your vision remains cloudy." The old professor steepled her fingers around the head of her cane. "You think the question is, do you love this man or not. Do you trust him? Do you give yourself to him? Do you bind your futures together?"

Kayla shaped the words with her mouth. But there was not enough air in the room to give them sound.

"I'm sorry, but this is not correct. You miss the core issue. The *real* choice is this." Dr. Beachley took a firmer grip on the cane and leaned in so close Kayla caught the rosewater scent of her powder. "The critical issue, my dear young lady, is whether you wish to renew *all* your passions. Do you choose to regain your zest for life? Do you desire to have the dross of bitter experiences turned to the gold of new beginnings? Do you seek the freedom to love anew?"

Kayla whispered, "How?"

Dr. Beachley leaned back, clearly satisfied. "An excellent starting point for your new assignment, wouldn't you agree?"

chapter 26

*F*ollowing the Bodleian luncheon, Adam dropped Peter off at the company and silently accepted the chairman's hoarse thanks. Adam remained deep within the adrenaline rush of a successful role. He drove back to the village where Honor greeted him with a hug, led him into Peter's office, delivered a tray of sandwiches and tea, and shut the door as she departed.

Adam pushed wearily through Derek Steen's downloaded files. By dinnertime he was certain they contained no direct reference to MVP's attack on Peter's company. Even so, the term *Serengeti* was everywhere, referred to in terse bullets that included such words as *crush, brutalize, bury*. Adam checked corporate listings in Europe and the United States, but could come up with nothing that used the Tanzanian name. The search kept him up until well after midnight. He would have stayed at it longer, but exhaustion swept him away. Adam barely made it up the stairs and into the guestroom bed.

He came grudgingly awake at a knock on his door. Honor stood in the alcove doorway, a steaming mug in her hand. "I let you sleep as long as I could."

"What time is it?"

"Almost ten." She entered the room and set the mug down on the side table. "Peter was hoping to speak with you before he meets with the executive committee this afternoon. And Professor Beachley phoned. She asked if you would stop by this morning. She made it sound quite urgent." Honor took a slip of paper from her pocket. "And Kayla asked me to give you this."

She handed him the note, then retreated to the doorway. "Adam, I hope you someday understand what your assistance has meant to Peter."

"He's a good man."

"Yes. He is that." Honor smiled. "Well, I'd best let you get dressed. Your breakfast is waiting."

Adam waited until the door closed behind her to unfold the slip of paper. Kayla's note read, *I went to church this morning. I prayed. For me. For you. For us. Love, K.*

The church door squeaked loudly as he let himself in. The sound echoed through the empty chamber. On the altar table, a single candle gleamed inside a lead crystal vase. Adam walked to the front pew and seated himself. In front of him was a waist-high frieze of intricately carved wood. Beyond it, a pair of stone steps rose to the altar and the table with its linen tablecloth. The cloth was embroidered with a crown of thorns surrounding a gold chalice.

He had spent a lifetime running from this place. It all came down to that. He had a million reasons to walk away. He caught a fragrance of incense as he slipped off the pew and came to rest upon the cold stone floor. He shut his eyes with the certainty he could not find his way alone.

That morning Kayla drove her father to the office. He had apparently rested well, for his voice was stronger and his features not so stained with exhaustion. Kayla allowed her father to escort her through his outer office as he would an honored guest. Mrs. Drummond served them coffee in the gold-rimmed china instead of the normal mugs. When they were alone, Peter said, "Honor told me of your desire to return the money. I won't hear of it. I don't wish to argue with you. So I'm asking that you set this notion aside."

She had a dozen reasons all lined up, ready to fire. But she did not have the heart to add to his strain. "All right, Daddy."

"Are we done with that?"

"If you insist."

"I do."

"Have you heard anything about yesterday's meeting?"

"Their response should be coming through later today." Peter coughed. "Adam was magnificent."

"So you told us last night. I wish I could have seen him."

"If we succeed in holding on to these investors, it will all be due to him."

"No, Daddy, I'm sorry. But that's not correct. He followed your lead."

His smile lacked the shadow she had been seeing since her return. "You're sure about that, are you?"

"Absolutely."

He hesitated, then asked, "You're still determined to return to Africa as planned?"

"I must." Suddenly the air carried a razorlike edge. "My ticket is booked. Tomorrow is your birthday. I leave the next morning."

She was terrified at what he might say. The slightest comment, the softest argument, and she knew her control would shatter. All the tears she had held back would come pouring out. And for a reason she would never have expected to find in this brief journey home.

But when Peter spoke, it was to say, "These past few days I have witnessed miracles with my own two eyes. Astounding events, joyful moments. The impossible made real. A young man who has been fired from my firm does everything within his power to keep this same company alive. My daughter joins me in our beloved church for the first time since her mother's funeral. And suddenly I find myself daring to voice a word I thought was lost to me."

Kayla waited until she was back in her little alcove before

she whispered the word for herself. But saying it softly was not enough. She took out a clean sheet of paper. She wrote down the word. She pinned it to the bulletin board. She sat there for quite some time, studying the word as she would a timeless mystery. *Hope.*

$\mathcal{A}$dam drove to Oxford and spent an hour with Professor Beachley. The previous day, the professor had met with the former student. She was now more adamant than ever that Adam was the answer to this young woman's crisis. Their discussion left Adam scarcely able to see the street back out to the corporate headquarters. His preoccupation carried him into the offices from which he had just been fired. A very curious receptionist told him to go straight to the chairman's office. Adam walked the long hall that carried him past the library and conference rooms and felt scrutiny from every quarter.

Mrs. Drummond was her normal unflappable self. "Mr. Austin will be with you directly." The chairman's secretary indicated Kayla's space. "Miss Austin asked me to give you her best, sir. She's off doing Christmas errands and said you might like to share her desk."

Adam glanced at the spot where he had first seen Kayla. "All right."

"If you'll excuse me for saying, sir, this is the first time Miss Austin has ever invited anyone into her alcove. You'd be well advised to find a proper means of saying thanks." Mrs. Drummond returned to her work. "Flowers might make for a nice start."

Adam seated himself and pulled out his two sets of notes, one from the previous evening's work and the others from his astonishing conversation with Dr. Beachley. Kayla's fragrance still lingered, a heady mixture of spices and distant lands. The desk was delicate and feminine, the edges carved into gentle waves. Adam then noticed the paper pinned to the board above the desk and it's single handwritten word, *Hope*. He sensed Kayla only left it because it was meant for them both.

"Mr. Wright? Mr. Austin will see you now."

Joshua Dobbins was seriously displeased to see Adam enter the chairman's office. "Really, Peter, this is most unwise."

"Your objections are duly noted." Peter waved Adam into a seat and declared hoarsely, "The colleges have elected to give us another six months to demonstrate a viable plan for recouping the lost earnings."

Adam felt a definable lightening of his body. As though he could suddenly cast aside the mental stones that had weighed down his hours. "That's an eternity."

"Not quite. But close enough from where I sit."

Joshua Dobbins protested, "This man has been dismissed."

"And I have hired him on my personal payroll. To work on a specific project."

"The board backed my decision!"

Peter Austin coughed, took a raspy breath, and said, "Old friend, we are poised on a knife's edge. I ask you to trust me. As you have so often in the past."

When Joshua subsided, Peter went on, "MVP has requested a meeting to discuss the acquisition of our firm."

"They must have heard about the colleges' decision to grant us more time," Adam said.

Joshua fumed, "Grant *us*?"

Peter glanced at his number two, then said, "I feel we should take the meeting. It may well buy us some breathing room."

Adam agreed, "They'll hold off trying to destroy you as long as they think there's a chance of buying the firm." He had a sudden thought. "Why not insist they ease the pressure being put on the Italian company that's brought you to the brink?"

Joshua said, "They'll deny all knowledge."

"It doesn't matter what they *say*. You heard Peter. We're after breathing room." Adam turned to the chairman. "Send Joshua. Put some space between you and the negotiations."

Peter cut off Joshua's protest before it could fully form. "Old friend, I have relied on you so often. It seems we are in need of your well-honed skills once again. Do not, I beg you, let us down."

When Joshua had departed, Peter said, "Joshua is not the spy."

"I know that."

"If there is one at all."

"I think he's correct. About MVP having a spy, and MVP being behind this crisis of ours."

"Joshua has been with me since the beginning. He is irascible, confrontational, often able to see only the potential risk. But I trust him implicitly."

Adam nodded, not so much in agreement as respect for this man and his ironclad principles. "I may have something. It could be nothing. But I think it's big."

Peter studied him across the expanse of his desk. "On what grounds?"

Adam extracted his second set of notes. "I have just had the most amazing meeting with Professor Beachley."

Adam drove them from the offices into the center of town. The sky brooded low over the city. The college's stone edifices frowned back at the sky and the passersby, gray and sullen. The streets were packed, particularly as they passed the Christmas markets. The front door of the last home on Norham Gardens Road opened before Adam cut the motor. The professor's smile of greeting defied the otherwise gloomy afternoon. "The past never seems more alive than in the faces of old friends."

Peter Austin bussed both cheeks. "You are very kind to a man who has ignored you for so long."

"Stuff and nonsense. Do come in and sit down." She thumped her way back into the front parlor. "I was just going to ring Mrs. Brandt for tea. Will you join me?"

"We don't want to be a bother."

"None of that. Adam, would you be so kind?"

When he returned, she directed him into a neighboring chair, then said to Peter, "Your young associate has impressed me to no end."

"You should have seen yesterday's performance."

"I am certain he did you proud."

When tea was served, Peter went on, "I really must apologize once more for not staying in touch, Sylvia."

"Oh, do be a good boy and let it be. You had lost your cherished wife. Anyone in their right mind would have known you were devastated by the loss. You did not need reminders like me hanging about. You needed to get on with life and be a father to your daughter." She erased the subject with a delicate gesture. "I must say, it was good to see your daughter looking so well. Kayla has a great deal of Amanda in her."

"That she does."

"Which, of course, makes her absence all the more difficult for you."

"Indeed, yes."

They took a distinctly English pause, an unspoken agreement between two old friends to set one topic aside and move on to another. Peter set his cup down on the table between them and said, "Perhaps you'd be kind enough to repeat for me what you told Adam this morning."

chapter 28

$\mathcal{R}$ain pattered softly against the French doors as Kayla
helped Honor prepare dinner. A fire crackled in the living room.
Two gentle melodies, rain and flames, nestling the home in a harmony of refuge and peace. When Peter and Adam had returned
an hour early, she had found herself observing Honor as much
as the men. This was how a woman in love greeted her man and
did her best to erase the stain of a hard day. This was how she
made her husband's new ally feel welcome. This was how she
cherished. This was how she gave. Yet as soon as Peter and Adam
retreated into the study, Honor seated herself at the kitchen table
and cradled her baby with both hands. Kayla did not ask if she
was all right. The words were not necessary. Kayla set the table,
and twice as she passed set a quick hand on Honor's shoulder.

When Honor finally rose and began helping her prepare
the salad, it felt the most natural thing in the world to give
voice to her thoughts. "Forgiveness is a major issue, isn't it?"

Honor's hand poised in the process of washing a head of
lettuce. "Of faith? Yes. Yes, it is."

"What if I can't?"

"None of us live up to the goal of perfection. But who knows, maybe you'll prove yourself wrong."

"I doubt that. Rather a lot, actually."

Honor reached for the dish towel and made a process of drying her hands. "It is amazing what the Spirit can do to a person. Even bringing a heartsick and angry young woman to the point where she could forgive both a father for destroying her life and a mother for pouring ashes over the remnant."

"But why bother?"

"That is the critical issue, isn't it? We become accustomed to living with pain and rage. It is what defines us. We might not like it. But it's the life we've been forced to claim as our own. So why change."

Kayla took the lettuce and began peeling off leaves, while Honor's words did the same to her internal state. Stripping away. One lie at a time.

"Then something happens. A problem we can't face alone. A need we can't fulfill. Something. And we have to go outside ourselves. Because if we don't, we lose the chance to grow beyond where we are. Not just for the moment. Forever. We are granted a glimpse into eternity's well. And we see that to drink from this means relinquishing things we both treasure and hate. Because it is the only way we can make room for the things we have denied ourselves."

Peter and Adam arrived at the dinner table in a reflective mood. Kayla watched Honor taste the air, then relax as she found no hint of latent stress. Abruptly Peter said, "Allow me to pose a hypothetical."

The entire table looked up, only to discover he was address-ing Adam, who said, "Fire away."

"Let us suppose for the moment that there could be a gradual influx of new funds for Kayla's project. Nothing immediately. But over time. How would you suggest she structure the change?"

Honor's eyes mirrored Kayla's surprise. Adam, however, seemed to find nothing unexpected in the question. He said, "Are we talking a fixed timeline?"

"Projected, but yes, all right. Let's say we would aim at a definite commitment."

Adam looked at Kayla. "Do you mind if I answer?"

"Do I mind? I don't even understand what either of you just said."

"How much do you need to get to profitability?" he asked her.

"You already know that. It costs us twelve thousand five hundred a month."

"No, Kayla. That's where you are *now*. It's how much you require to function. What I need to know is, what would be the bare minimum required to get you running at a point where income covers costs."

"Everything depends upon the drought."

Adam remained silent as he studied the notes beside his plate. Finally he said to Peter, "The first task would have to be establishing a new business plan. Kayla's financial structure is probably still based on before the double crisis of drought and robbery. So she's got all these commitments still based on projects that were left half-finished."

Peter asked, "Is he right?"

"Is he . . . I don't . . ." She stopped. Took a breath. "Yes, I suppose he is. Partly."

"Go on, Adam."

"My guess is, the fake business manager told her to jump into everything at once. That was the only way he could be certain to get all the capital down to Africa, where he could steal it. Force her to dive into the deep end. He expected her to drown. Instead, she's defied the odds and kept this thing going."

Kayla exchanged another look with Honor. This was more than just a casual discussion. Or so it sounded to her. Kayla asked, "Are we talking theoretical?"

Peter coughed, but the previous day's wheeze was absent. "Allow our young friend to finish."

Adam said, "I would stagger the projects."

"Starting with what?"

He turned back to Kayla. "What is your biggest money-maker?"

That did not require any thought. "Coffee. The growers have been there for generations. The supermarkets already have the space available for Fair Trade coffee."

"What further investment does your coffee division need at present?"

"A new roaster. Two more trucks. Better sorting mechanisms. Equipment for the new start-up villages. Many other villages need deeper irrigation wells. A full-time coordinator to maintain quality during the growing season." She had to fight for breath. "What—"

"So the coffee is covered. What would be next?"

She forced her mind to work. Or tried. "The biggest money-maker after coffee is cut flowers. Especially in the winter."

"What about the drought?"

"One portion of the country has an excellent underground aquifer. And there are two lakes that haven't gone dry. We need irrigation pumps and tents that trap the water and keep it from evaporation. Israel has invented a desert-style irrigation system that drips water directly onto each plant, wasting almost nothing."

Adam said to Peter, "The study would have to be double-bound. There's the profitability issue per product, and you'd have to determine how many villages benefit per dollar invested."

"What if the lost capital could be replaced all at once?" Peter asked.

"I'd still urge her to stagger things out. Each of these is going to generate a ton of new work. There's the issue of personnel, of keeping things in harmony, working with the buyers, regulating quality and output so she can guarantee a regular supply . . ."

Honor broke in with, "Something's happened, hasn't it?"

The two men exchanged a glance before Peter replied, "The answer, my dear, is that we simply do not know."

Kayla asked, "Can you tell me anything?"

Her father said, "Soon."

"Adam?"

"Hi, Mom."

"What time is it?"

"Just after eight your time. Around one in the morning over here."

"Couldn't you sleep?"

"I'm supposed to be the one asking you that."

"I sleep too much."

"So you can sleep for the two of us." Adam carried the phone back into the living room. He had woken from a deep sleep and instantly known he would be up for a while. He settled into a chair before the cold fireplace. He refrained from asking how she was doing. His mother hated that question. If he had to know, he would ask the nurses. But their answers were always the same by now. His mother was doing as well as could be expected. She was without pain. She was a wonderful patient, a blessing to everyone at the hospice. Adam had heard the comments so often he could recite them at will.

His mother asked, "So how are things?"

This was a good sign. On her not-so-good days, his mother's interests were reduced to a quick hello, a sighed thanks that he phoned, an assurance of her love, and off again. "Things are really good."

"I'm so glad. Tell me about England."

"It's cold here. The weather changes from hour to hour. The winter sun only rises about an inch above the horizon, and seems to skirt the treetops as it moves from east to west."

"But it's beautiful?"

"Yes, Mom." At the sound of a creaking floorboard, Adam turned to find Kayla standing hesitantly in the foyer. She wore a quilted robe over gray flannel pajamas. Her hair was tousled and her feet bare. She had never looked more lovely. "Hang on just a second, Mom."

Kayla said, "I thought I heard your voice."

"Come on in."

"I don't want to disturb."

"You're not. Really."

"Would you like a hot chocolate?"

"Sure." He lifted the receiver. "Okay, Mom. I'm back."

"Who was that?"

"A friend."

"You've made friends already?"

"Yes. Good ones."

"I'm so glad."

"Have you had any more dreams?"

"Perhaps the time for dreaming is over."

His next breath came with difficulty. "What makes you say that?"

Kayla must have heard the change, for she padded back into the room and rested her hand upon his shoulder.

His mother said, "I seem to come and go these days. I can hardly recall what we spoke about last time. The dreams, from where I lay, they seem like idle musings."

"No, Mom. They were important."

"Were they?"

"Very."

"Then perhaps they were never intended for me at all."

He felt a building pressure, a need to know so strong he

pushed out the words, "Your first dream about me needing to travel to England came after I apologized. You said I needed to figure out why you sent me—"

"I did not send you, Adam. I felt that you were being called to go. Only you refused to accept the *concept* of being called."

Adam took a firmer hold of Kayla's hand. "I understand."

"Do you really?"

"I think so."

"Then everything is right in this old world of mine." His mother's breathing came in soft puffs, as though each required a special effort. "I think I had better rest. I love you, Adam."

When he looked up, Kayla's gaze held a depth and a calm as piercing as the night. She reached down and enfolded him in her arms. The quilted robe softened her embrace and blanketed his vision.

$\mathcal{K}$ayla was lifted from dreamless slumber by Honor's soft knock upon the door. She rose and dressed and joined them downstairs in the kitchen. She could hear Adam's footsteps creaking the floor overhead. Her father and Honor gave her soft morning embraces and poured her a coffee. She wished her father a happy birthday and smiled as Honor told Peter of her birthday gift, a weekend getaway to Paris. She could see how hard her father tried to be pleased and grateful for his wife.

Adam came into the kitchen, his gaze still hollowed by the midnight conversation with his mother. Kayla found it the most natural thing in the world to walk over to him and fit herself into his arms. Her father and Honor looked over and smiled.

The morning service was a soft song of hope. When the prayers began, Adam slipped off the pew to kneel upon the cold stone floor. Kayla took one of the padded cushions off the little brass hook, set it on the floor, and knelt beside him. Her mind returned to the night before and the image of a strong man made weak. She prayed for Adam's mother. She prayed for Adam. She prayed for her father and for Honor and for the baby and for the business. Quick images of a phrase, a few words, flowing now from an overfull heart. Her single prayer for herself was equally brief, equally natural: *Help me hope again.*

She stopped praying when her father's hand settled upon her shoulder, and she was filled with the sense that she truly, finally, had come home.

They opened their front door to the sound of the ringing phone. Her father lifted the receiver. "Hello? Ah, Sylvia. How very nice of you to phone."

Kayla asked, "Is that Professor Beachley?"

Honor asked, "Who?"

Adam held up one hand. Wait.

Peter's breathing rasped loudly in the silent house. "No, I quite understand. According to what you told us yesterday, the lady and her companions have been badly scarred. They have every right to be concerned. Of course I'll travel down. Naturally Adam will accompany me. No, don't apologize. I am most grateful that you would seek to make this happen."

He set down the receiver, coughed once more, then said to Adam, "Sylvia has managed to make us an appointment. But she does not hold out much hope."

Kayla glanced at Adam and was surprised to see how his face reflected her father's expression, an equal mix of tension and expectation. Adam turned to her and said, "We might have a new deal in the works."

Kayla said, "What you wouldn't tell us about last night."

Adam waited through a half-dozen heartbeats. Peter's gaze remained steady on the younger man. Adam said, "There's a problem. We need to go into this meeting with our money at the ready. But the way things stand, there's a risk Joshua would block an outlay of more funds."

Honor said, "That man again."

Kayla understood. "You need my money."

"It's a lot to ask. You have every right to say no."

Kayla felt the past rise up to strike her anew. Another man wanting to take her last real chance of survival. She saw her father shake his head. Knew she could give voice to his gesture and be completely within her rights.

She asked, "How much?"

Adam's face was a mirror of her father's solemnity. "All of it."

Though Reading was a mere half-hour's drive south of Oxford, the two cities could not have been any different. Reading was a city scourged by industrial neglect and poverty. Derelict mills sprouted from row after row of brownstone squalor. The central thoroughfare swept them past a Victorian prison of brick and fortress towers and hopelessness. The University of Reading occupied a cluster of buildings south of the city center. The traffic was sullen and aggressive. Adam finally gave up his hunt for a parking space and left the Mercedes in the faculty lot. A parking ticket was the least of this day's risks.

The biochemistry lab was a charmless redbrick structure over a hundred years old. Alongside it was an unfinished structure of mirrored glass and concrete and construction clamor. Inside the old building a sign announced that the single elevator was broken. Following Dr. Beachley's instructions, they took the stairs to the third floor. Fluorescent lights hung from crumbling ceilings. Glass-fronted labs revealed state-of-the-art machinery resting on antique lab tables. Students flowed about them in a noisy din.

Their destination was a lab crammed into the far northeast corner. Two of the windows did not shut completely, so the first sound that greeted their arrival was a faint whistling draft. No one spoke as Peter knocked on the partly open door. Three white-coated scientists worked in a chaotic tangle. Boxes were piled everywhere.

Peter asked, "Dr. Hao Ping?"

A diminutive Asian in a lab coat straightened from piling papers into a carton. "You're Mr. Austin?"

A woman with skin the color of strong tea and a lilting Indian accent said, "We happen to be very busy here today."

The third person, a woman with a rat's nest of red hair and thick glasses, protested, "Dr. Beachley said this was important."

"She said it might possibly be important," Hao Ping corrected.

The Indian lady typed upon the computer keyboard with unnecessary force. "I am pushing extremely hard, trying to finish these calculations before we are shut down."

The redheaded scientist said, "If what Dr. Beachley told us is correct—"

"Dr. Beachley, Dr. Beachley, it's all I hear from you these days."

"—your rushing about might not be necessary anymore."

"If we could rely on this Dr. Beachley, she would have found us space at Oxford."

The redheaded lady sighed and went back to packing her box.

The young man turned to his two cohorts. "So do we speak with them or not?"

"Not," the lady at the computer said. "You let these people in the door, and soon they are prying away at secrets we do not need to be sharing."

The young man looked uncertain. The redhead kept packing her box.

Peter said gently, "Sometimes the hardest thing in the world is to determine the difference between what is real hope and what is just another failure in the making."

The Indian lady slowed her furious typing. The redheaded scientist turned from her box.

"But that is what makes for successful science, does it not? Pursuing in the face of repeated failure, until the winning formula has been realized."

The Indian lady remained staring into the screen. Her features slackened into an expression of weary resignation.

The redheaded scientist said, "Let them in, Hao."

They gathered in an office scarcely large enough for the desk, the crates, and two straight-backed chairs. They somehow managed to cram everyone inside, but only by having the two lady scientists lean against the windowsill, flanking Hao Ping, who was seated behind the desk. The English scientist asked, "How much do you know?"

"Dr. Beachley explained that you were being denied both funding and the chance to continue your research here at Reading."

"They're using the transfer to the new labs as an excuse to shut us down," Hao Ping confirmed.

"Might I ask your names?"

"This is Ms. Kamuran and Ms. Haine. They should both be postdocs by now, but their theses have been turned down by the university review board."

The Indian scientist demanded, "Didn't your precious Sylvia tell you about that too?"

"Orla," the other woman said. "Please."

"She mentioned that there had been a problem with your thesis adviser," Peter confirmed. "And that in her opinion the entire affair was a monstrous injustice."

Ms. Haine motioned to a pair of boxes beneath the constantly whistling window. "Our latest results are in those three boxes."

The Indian lady was not so easily mollified. "This data can't leave the office."

"Orla, you can't ask them to—"

"This whole thing is a charade. It's just more people I don't know, mucking about with my life's work."

"Our work," the young man corrected. "I've been here the whole time, remember?"

The Indian lady did not respond.

Ms. Haine went on, "Hao has lost his lectureship defending us and our theses."

Hao said to them, "Seven years we've been working on this project."

The Indian lady said, "The data stays here."

Ms. Haine sighed and looked out the window.

Peter's chair creaked as he shifted his weight. "Let me see if I have this in proper perspective. Seven years ago, you began work with sea snails. Why? Because their secretions are so strong their prey remain utterly relaxed and dormant, even while the snail's digestive juices literally eat them alive. The enzyme responsible had been studied before, and right here in this very university."

Adam marveled at this man. Peter's breathing was a harsh testimony to months of burdens and worries. His features were aged and puffy. Yet his essential goodness came through, such that the three scientists gradually emerged from behind their hostile barriers.

Hao said, "This initial work was done by the head of our department."

The English scientist said, "He also discovered that the enzyme was highly toxic to humans."

The Indian lady said, "And he built his reputation on this work."

Peter nodded solemn agreement. "But using new molecular techniques, which were not available to your department head when he did his original research, you made a significant discovery. That was last year sometime, was it not?"

Hao Ping replied, "This past January."

"Which is most interesting, as it more or less parallels the beginning of your own difficulties." Peter smiled at their silence, as though he could not have hoped for a better response. "You managed to dissect the enzyme, which according to Dr. Beachley is a singular feat. You removed the toxic particle."

"We've been working on this for five years," Ms. Haine said. "Removing one particle after another until the danger was eradicated."

Peter went on, "And what you have as a result of your diligent work is a powerful new painkiller. One so potent it removes all sensation entirely, yet your test subjects remained fully conscious. These are astounding results."

The Indian lady said, "Not according to our department's funding committee."

"Hardly a surprise, since your work overturns the major lifetime achievement of your department head." Peter let the silence hang for a moment, then said, "This is as far as we got with Dr. Beachley. Perhaps you would be so kind as to continue?"

The three scientists exchanged a long glance. There must have been some silent accord, because Hao Ping turned back around and said, "We went to the university lawyer, who put us in touch with some venture people."

"Venture capitalists," Ms. Haine corrected. "City types."

"Might I inquire of their name?"

"Madden and Van Pater."

Adam had the sense of being jolted out of his chair. He knew that bodily he was still seated. But some component of his awareness lifted clear of his physical reality and bolted about the room.

Peter, on the other hand, merely bowed his head.

Ms. Kamuran asked, "Do you know them?"

"So well," Peter replied, "I can probably describe the scenario you have faced."

The Indian scientist said, "Go on, then."

He raised his head. "MVP expressed an initial interest. They demanded data and more data. They dithered."

When the two scientists turned toward Ms. Haine, she protested, "Don't look at me, I didn't tell Dr. Beachley any of this."

"It's a favorite tactic when dealing with nonbusiness types. They dangled the prospect of major funding just out of reach and in the process caught a glimpse of just how dire was your need. Once that was revealed, their pessimism began to grow. They apologized profusely, but said they couldn't take on such an enormous risk without your first giving up a majority share. And once you agreed to that, the stake they offered you began to shrink."

By this point, all three scientists were gaping openly at Peter, who went on, "And all the while, no money has actually appeared."

Ms. Kamuran demanded, "How do you know?"

Peter glanced at Adam. "Perhaps you would be so good as to explain."

Adam laid it all out. From the beginning to now. Including the destruction of Kayla's project.

When he was done, the office was silent except for the softly shrieking wind. Finally Ms. Kamuran asked, "How do we know you are any different?"

Peter asked, "Is your product truly as good as Sylvia indicated?"

The English scientist gestured to the boxes. "Our lab reports clearly document—"

"Forgive me, Ms. Haine. For the moment, set the statistical results to one side. As they say in my trade, let us please cut to the bottom line."

Again the trio exchanged a glance. This time, the Indian scientist said, "Tell them."

Hao Ping said, "Our discovery is as strong as morphine, but does not affect the cognitive processes. The subject remains entirely alert, but simply no longer feels pain at whatever point of the body has received the injection. There are no side effects. Nor are there any lingering traces. The body breaks down the drug as it would any other naturally produced enzyme. In summary, this could well mark a turning point in the treatment of chronic pain."

Ms. Haine said, "We need to move to human trials."

"Of course you do." Peter extracted an envelope from his side pocket. "This is the only way I know to demonstrate the difference between MVP and ourselves."

Hao Ping opened the envelope and read the check, "Two hundred thousand pounds."

Adam stared at the check in the scientist's hands and repressed a smile over the irony of using Steen's own money against the company who had employed him as a thief.

"We are currently working with a company that specializes in human trials. They have labs attached to the Radcliffe Hospital. You must, of course, verify your findings with their board of governors, but if they agree, the company will represent you in seeking government approval."

The Indian lady asked weakly, "When?"

"The approval process can take months."

"No. When will they make the application?"

"I spoke with the director this morning. Assuming your documentation is in order and your product lives up to your claims, they will begin the paperwork this afternoon and make the official governmental application next week."

Hao Ping said numbly, "Next *week?*"

"Seven years," Ms. Haine murmured.

Ms. Kamuran asked, "In exchange for what?"

"We will take half of your company's ownership plus one percent," Peter replied. "We would hope to go public in six months or less. In the meantime, you are welcome to continue packing."

Hao Ping asked, "Where are we going?"

"Oh, didn't I say? The director assures me your lab space will be ready by this afternoon."

chapter 30

*A*dam drove through the company's tall front gates and spun softly around the forecourt. He came to rest by a massive oak with the Mercedes' snout pointed back toward the exit. The wind now carried rain mixed with snow and frozen pellets that bounced off the hood. Kayla scampered down the front steps, climbed into the rear seat, and demanded, "Tell me what happened."

Peter nodded to Adam, who related the outcome of their meeting. When he finished, Kayla sat in silence. The motor purred. The heater sighed softly. The dashboard clock ticked off the moments. The rain fell.

Kayla said, "This application process and human trials could take months."

"Years, more like."

"But you're certain this untested product will give Daddy the leverage he needs?"

"This isn't about bringing the product to market," Adam replied. "It's the *potential*. All they need is a product with the *potential* to be a headline grabber. The lab company that was such a drain on our resources suddenly becomes a huge draw for major drug firms. They'll be lining up to place bids."

"You gave them Derek's money?"

"It's not Derek's, it's yours," Adam quietly corrected. "We couldn't have done this without your help."

"He's not exaggerating, my dear," Peter confirmed. "What an extraordinary gesture you've made. In this dire hour, you've helped shape an answer to prayer. Both of you. I can't thank you two enough."

Peter opened his door. "I shall go inform Joshua and the board. Adam, perhaps it would be best if you stayed out here. No need to wave the red flag in his face."

"I need to go tell Dr. Beachley what's happened."

"I'll go with him," Kayla said.

"Do tell her I shall be around directly to thank her personally."

They watched Peter disappear into the company headquarters. Kayla slipped from the rear into the seat beside Adam. She studied his profile in the faded gray of a rain-swept day. What was it the professor had called him? "The wounded hero." She saw the man's strength, felt it in the warmth that encircled her hand. And saw his weaknesses as well.

Derek's image came to mind then. No longer Geoffrey, the fable now firmly banished. Adam might still have the capacity to *act* the thief. But Kayla knew the true capacity to *be* a heartless robber of dreams was no longer real. Derek had never been capable of admitting weakness. Any question that threatened him was deflected with a laugh, a joke, a false embrace. And it was false, all of it. Yet as she examined these facts, Kayla sensed a difference in herself. This time, in accepting that she had been blinded, she also admitted that she had *wanted* to be blind. It was not merely that Derek had lied to her. Kayla had *helped* him. The falsehood had been complete only because she had wanted it so.

She blinked, and in so doing washed away Derek's image. Such a simple act. One moment there, the next gone, and this time without the aching void at the center of her being.

Kayla reached over and gripped Adam's hand. She recalled that morning's prayer. *Help me to hope again.* She wondered if the moment's flavor was how forgiveness tasted.

Adam said softly, "I need to go back to America. I don't care what Mom says or thinks or dreams. I need to be there for her."

Kayla nodded agreement. Adam licked his lips. He tried to speak. To ask the impossible. But could not find the strength.

Kayla knew the words as clearly as though he had spoken them aloud. She felt herself falling into that gaze, so deep she could read the invitation and find the strength to ask, "Would you like me to come with you?"

chapter 31

When they returned from Norham Gardens Road, Kayla went into the company offices to fetch her father. Adam thought Kayla had never looked more beautiful than she did that afternoon, walking with her father down the company's front stairs. Oh, she might have been more elegant at one time or another. Her hair might have been done by a London stylist, and a beautician might have painted her features to perfection. Armani might have produced her dress and Jimmy Choo her heels. But no manufactured myth would ever hold Adam as she did now, walking through a gray afternoon, the rain slipping softly into snow.

Which was a silly reason to be smiling and reaching for her when she entered the car. But her smile told him it was all right. And maybe even better than that.

Peter slipped into the rear seat and announced, "The board did not exactly fling their arms and declare my project the deliverance we've all been hoping for."

"But they backed you," Adam said.

"It was a close run thing. But they agreed to hold all further actions until the new year. Joshua was most displeased."

271

Kayla settled her hand upon Adam's shoulder, up where she could trace one finger along Adam's neck. "Good."

Peter smiled and said, "I have instructed our bank to transfer the funds back into Kayla's account. They should be in place before the close of the day."

"Thank you, Daddy." Kayla turned far enough around to look her father in the eye and say, "Let's go home and celebrate your birthday."

The snow swept in, and with it came the wind. Their world became limited to the first few cars before them and the headlights immediately behind. As Adam turned onto the main road headed out of town, Peter said, "I regret that I was unable to convince the board that you should be immediately reinstated. I fought them rather hard on that point. But they were insistent. No doubt I shall have better luck at the January meeting."

Adam felt Kayla's gaze on him. He knew she was mulling something over. The weight of her thoughts carried across the pair of seats and lodged in his skin where she stroked him.

"In the meantime," Peter said, "I'd be grateful if you would continue assisting me in an unofficial capacity. It's hardly fair, given the role you've played in this turnaround. And you will be compensated. I can assure you—"

"Daddy."

"Yes, my dear?"

"Adam isn't doing this for the money." She continued to watch him. "Are you?"

"No."

"Of course, I understand. But I would still like to see you rewarded for your efforts."

"I am. A hundred times over."

"As your first responsibility, I would like you to help me structure a new division. I am thinking we should name it Legacy. We need a definable structure for future projects. I've been altogether too haphazard in the past. The company does not even have a fixed amount of our budget designated for these projects. We need to create a definable structure within which to operate."

Adam said, "That's a great idea."

"I'm so very glad you approve."

Kayla turned slightly in her seat. "Adam needs to go see his mother."

"Well, of course—"

"I've agreed to go with him. We will leave tomorrow. I'll fly straight from Washington back to Dar es Salaam."

Peter's only response was to watch Kayla's hand upon Adam's shoulder. The snowstorm disappeared just as they passed the Ring Road and entered the first layer of hills. Overhead, the leaden gray was whipped to froth. Peter's gaze remained on his daughter's hand and the finger that traced its way back and forth along Adam's hairline. He said, "I do believe this is going to be the finest birthday I have ever had."

Adam watched the next snow flurry bear down on them. It pelted sideways, driven with the force of frozen white nails. Ahead of him, lighter cars jerked as the deeper puddles shoved them about. The Mercedes, however, belonged to an era when cars were built without regard to weight or aerodynamics. Even in this storm, Adam maintained control with a light touch.

Five minutes the deluge lasted, then it was gone, leaving behind a sky that was not so much gray as void. Adam turned onto the smaller country road. Around him, treetops waved in excited unison. Adam took a breath so deep his ribs popped. The air was spiced with Kayla's fragrance and the heady scent of a better tomorrow.

Peter's phone chirped. He answered, and though Adam could not hear the words, he knew from the way the man's features softened that he spoke with Honor. The country lane bundled around a curve, then passed a rise, then swept down to run alongside the storm-swollen river. Peter cut off his phone and stowed it back in his pocket. Adam spotted the next squall approaching from his right. The tempest stalked across the windswept ridgeline on a billion legs of white and gray. There were no other cars now, just him and the empty road. Adam pressed down on the accelerator, aiming to make the curve and enter the long straightaway before the snow masked his vision.

The snow struck just as he completed the turn. And with it came the sound of thunder. Or so it seemed.

The other car appeared with such suddenness, Adam's first thought was that it had been molded from the storm. The beast of steel and raging speed bounded down the steep farm lane, racing so fast all four wheels pitched off the surface.

As Adam's foot was already on the accelerator, he mashed it to the floor. That simple act, taken with instinctive confidence in his vehicle, saved them. "Watch out!"

Kayla gripped his shoulder with one hand and the dash with her other. But Peter was in the process of stowing away his phone and faced the opposite direction.

The Mercedes' eight cylinders bellowed with a desperate desire to reach safety. And they almost did. The oncoming car did not hit them dead center, as was intended. Instead, it struck just behind Peter's door. Despite her double-handed grip, the force punched Kayla into Adam's chest. Peter's forehead splintered the nearside window, then he bounced the entire way across the car to land in the footwell behind Adam's seat.

Adam was rigid with the effort to maintain both his death grip on the steering wheel and keep the accelerator jammed to the floorboards. The rear tires slewed on the slick pavement, then lost traction entirely.

The attacker gunned his engine so high it forced the Mercedes to vibrate in frantic unison. Adam kept his own foot jammed all the way down. The Mercedes' wheels shrieked a panic note. The car filled with the smell of burning rubber.

A sudden gust blew down the valley, clearing the space between the two cars. Adam stared through the attacker's snow-streaked windscreen. Derek Steen glared back at him, his face twisted in a screaming frenzy.

The massive car had been caught at a terrible angle. The country lane was not just narrow. It had no verge. As soon as the spinning wheels left the wet asphalt and touched the grass, Adam might as well have sought to drive on air.

Derek's car had the double advantage of momentum and traction. Derek pushed and kept pushing as the Mercedes slewed violently. It seemed to Adam like the car tipped in impossibly slow motion, as though the car tried to fight to save them. Tried and failed.

Adam's final glimpse of their attacker was Derek Steen shouting in triumphant rage as the Mercedes gave way.

The car tilted over the ledge. The angle deepened. Kayla screamed something he could not manage to hear. The leading wheels struck an indentation in the riverbank.

The car flipped over entirely.

The roof crashed into the river running alongside the road. The rain-thickened waters beat through Peter's shattered window. The car began to settle.

Water hissed in a frigid murky jet straight into Adam's face. He untangled Kayla from his chest. She had gone completely still. It took forever to undo his seat belt. Kayla was not moving. Adam took a breath and submerged down to where his face was within inches of her seat belt's clip. He tugged and wrenched and finally managed to free her.

Only when he came up gasping did he feel the cold slice his face.

"Kayla!"

She might have spoken a word. But it came out disjointed and tainted by her moan.

"Kayla, I need you!" He gripped her arms and shook her harder than he intended, because her head bounced on the seat cushion, which was now the roof. Her eyes came fully open, though. Adam moved in close enough to fill her field of vision. "Your father needs help."

"Daddy?"

"Focus, Kayla. We've got to get out of here."

"What happened . . . Daddy?"

Adam scrambled around so that his knees rested on the steering wheel. "See if you can crank the window open."

He pushed himself back through the frigid murk. Peter sprawled across the rear, his head wedged between the ledge and the rear window. Which meant he had remained clear of the inrushing water. "Peter!"

Blood washed in a dirty pink stream from a cut above his temple. It was the only color to his features. His eyelids flickered. "Peter, you've got to wake up!"

Behind him he heard rhythmic thumps as Kayla worked on a door. "It's stuck partway!"

Adam felt the car shift upon the riverbed and sink another six inches. "Can you make it out?"

"It's very narrow . . . What about Daddy?"

"Get to the bank and be ready to take him!" If the opening was narrow, Adam would not be able to manhandle Peter through it. He braced himself on the opposite door and began kicking at the broken side window. The Mercedes had settled at an angle that left the smashed window at a slight upward angle. Adam fought against the inrushing water and carefully kicked away all the remnants of glass that he could find. He gripped Peter's jacket with one hand, and with the other clenched the carpet covering the drive train directly overhead. He wedged himself through the open window as far as he could go and still keep his face and Peter's clear of the water. Then a deep breath. Another. Adam ducked under the water and pried himself through the window, dragging Peter along with him.

Peter's shoulders jammed tight. Adam shouted into the rushing stream, mashed one shoulder back, and pulled the other forward. Peter shot through the window as though ejected.

A branch raked the back of his neck. Adam heard his shirt rip. Furiously he fought off the limb and pulled Peter up to where his face cleared the water.

Adam came up gasping. The torrent clutched at him as he dragged Peter toward the shore. Falling snow and ice pelted him. Kayla appeared alongside him and helped drag Peter up the muddy, slippery embankment.

Only when they hit the level grass verge at the top did Adam give in to the tremors.

Kayla cradled her father's head and blew into his mouth. Adam pushed himself to his feet. It was a dreadfully long process. His legs felt as though they belonged to someone else, a man without the brain function to instruct them properly.

He looked down. Kayla shivered and pushed at her father's chest and then breathed into his mouth. She pushed again. And breathed once more.

Peter coughed. Sputtered. Coughed again.

Adam tried to say, "I'm going for help." The words were so mangled he did not understand them himself. But Kayla looked up at him, blinked through the snow flaking her eyelashes, and nodded.

Adam stumbled down the road. He looked back at the curve. The snow already obliterated Kayla, her father, and the river.

The walk took forever. He almost went down twice.

Only when he reached the highway did Adam realize he was shouting at the storm. A wordless barrage, willing his body to fight through.

He was yelling so loud he did not hear the truck until it was almost on top of him. The driver frantically mashed on the brakes as the rear end slewed slightly. Adam stumbled out of the way and went down. The behemoth shuddered to a halt just as he managed to make his feet again. The cab's door opened and a voice shouted through the storm, "If that ain't your blood, mate, it will be soon enough!"

chapter 32

*A*dam found it somehow fitting to have Officer Walton enter the hospital waiting room the same moment as Joshua. The company financial officer looked weak and insubstantial next to the uniformed policewoman.

The local Oxford constable who had been interviewing Adam asked, "Is Scotland Yard taking an interest in this case?"

"In a manner of speaking." She offered Adam her hand. "How are you?"

Bruised. Sore. Still cold at some level far below his now-dry skin. Even so, Adam was glad enough to be there to answer, "Fine."

"And your mates?"

"The doctors say Peter probably suffered a concussion, but the scan didn't show any internal bleeding or abnormal swelling. Twenty stitches in his forehead and a possible dislocated shoulder. But he's resting well."

"And your lady friend?"

"Kayla is in with her father."

"Sounds like you came out the hero."

The local Oxford policeman cleared his throat. "We were in the process of establishing that."

Officer Walton nodded in Adam's direction. "Take it from me. This is one of the good guys."

"You're certain about that, are you?"

"As a matter of fact, I am." She pulled over a chair. "Appreciate the call."

"Glad you were there to take it."

The trucker had proven to be a good guy, once he was certain Adam's plight was real. He pulled his rig down the lane, settled Peter between the seats and bundled Kayla into the crawl space behind them. He turned the cab's heater up to toasty and made record time back to Oxford. He even let Adam use his phone, first to call ahead to the hospital, and then Honor. The only time the trucker had shown a hint of alarm was when Adam asked information to pass him through to Scotland Yard.

Officer Walton examined the surgical scrubs he wore and gave him a cop's smile, a faint tightening of the eyes. "You look good in blue."

"At least it's dry."

She noticed Joshua hovering in the background and asked, "Are you with this gentleman?"

When Joshua hesitated, Adam said, "Yes. He is."

Officer Walton turned back and reported, "Derek Steen was apprehended at Heathrow Airport, in the process of boarding a flight to Manila."

"First long-haul flight out of town."

"No doubt. I stopped by Heathrow on the way out. The offer

to extradite him back to a cozy African cell worked wonders. As they say in your neck of the woods, he sang like a parrot."

"The correct term," Adam said, "is canary."

"It so happens he was fired by his company, what's it called?"

Adam looked at Joshua. "Madden and Van Pater."

"That's the one. Took it hard, our lad did. He seemed delighted with my interest in how they sent him down to that place . . ."

Adam kept his gaze on the tightly clenched accountant. "Dar es Salaam."

"He's confessed that he stole your lady friend's missing funds. At the company's instructions, apparently. I was hoping you might be able to clear up the issue of motive for me."

"MVP has been gunning for Peter's company since he left them fifteen years ago."

Joshua cleared his throat. "Actually, it was sixteen."

"MVP is Steen's former employer?"

"That's how they're known in the City." Adam recounted what they had learned.

Officer Walton extracted a notebook and pen and took swift notes. "So MVP saw Ms. Austin's project as another means by which Oxford Ventures was establishing itself within the colleges and their investment capital."

"Basically."

"I'll need to pass this by my colleagues in the Fraud Division. But my guess is, MVP is soon going to be far too busy with their own troubles to mess with you again." She rose to her feet and said to the Oxford cop, "Why don't we go have a word with Ms. Austin, see if she corroborates his story."

Adam asked, "What about Derek?"

"Mr. Steen requested an attorney, which was of course his privilege. He's been remanded into Her Majesty's custody and carted downtown. We'll give the lad a night alone in a cell while I meet with my mates in Fraud. Then the lot of us will all sit down and see what kind of deal we can work out." She gave him another cop's smile. "My guess is, the prospect of seeing prison in fine Salaambay will have him hitting the high notes."

Joshua Dobbins stepped in close enough to reveal a slight tick over his left eye. "I gather you're expecting me to apologize."

"Not really, no."

"I did what I thought was best for the company."

"My only argument with you," Adam said, "was that you didn't back Peter's play."

"He's always been too emotional. Too involved in looking beyond profits."

"Too determined to make his company into something more than MVP," Adam finished. "Something greater. A firm with a higher ideal than simply making money."

Joshua wanted to shut him down. The bitter taste of speaking with Adam at all twisted his mouth and pinched his face. "Peter has regularly allowed his enthusiasms to run away from him. My job was to keep the worst of these crazes from taking us down."

Adam decided there was nothing to be gained by arguing the point further. "I've been preparing a list of possible deals where they've skirted the law. The folder is marked 'Steen.' There's a copy in the bottom drawer of Peter's home office desk."

Joshua glanced toward the doors. But when they opened to admit Mrs. Drummond and not the police, he turned back and said, "Your friend at Scotland Yard intimated they would not be bothering us again."

Mrs. Drummond glanced uncertainly around the waiting room, then slipped out the door again. Adam said, "Whether or not the police find enough evidence to make a case, it's all going to take time. And time is the one thing we can't afford to give MVP. We need to get them off our back."

Reluctantly Joshua nodded agreement. "How . . ."

"I hired a detective to scope out MVP. I used my funds and did it independent of the company. What you have comes from one source, not board level. I found nothing directly related to the attack on us. But there are numerous memos related to some project called Serengeti." Adam related his confrontation with Madden at the luncheon.

Joshua mulled that over. "It must be code for some illegal project."

Then Kayla entered the waiting room with Mrs. Drummond in tow. "Adam, we need to speak. It's urgent."

Joshua rose to his feet, hesitated, then offered Adam his hand. "Will I be seeing you around?"

Adam shook his hand, replied, "Count on it."

Joshua held his hand a fraction longer than necessary, and said simply, "Good."

Kayla remained stationed by the exit until she had glared Joshua through the doors. When she moved forward, Adam asked, "How's your father?"

"Resting."

"Did you talk to the police?"

"Yes." She sat down and took his hand. "Adam, something's happened to your mother. When the hospice couldn't raise you on your phone or at the boardinghouse, they called the office." Kayla added her other hand to the mix. "It doesn't look good."

$\mathscr{A}$t Heathrow's Terminal Three, Honor embraced first Kayla and then Adam. She wished them a good flight and said she and Peter had decided to put off the birthday celebration and Christmas so the four of them could enjoy it together. She then whispered something to Kayla, who nodded and embraced her once more in reply.

Adam waved at the vanishing car and wondered at the ease this family had with farewells and sudden journeys. He asked, "Do you want to tell me what she said?"

Kayla bit her lip, then said, "If at all possible, either she or Peter will be there when your mother's time comes."

Adam passed through Heathrow departures in a calm that was maintained only because of his traveling companion. Beside him, Kayla might have been suffering from an overdose of worry and haste on top of her bruises, but he would never tell from looking at her. She appeared utterly unfazed by the entire process, checking in, passport control, the stepped-up security, the garish duty-free hall, the noise, the crush, the call for their flight. The plane left from Terminal Three's farthest gate, a long trek down a tunnel enclosed by glass and rain.

He and Kayla slept, her head resting upon his shoulder most of the way across the Atlantic. He listened to the plane drone above the wintry sea, his vision clouded by the veil of her hair. When Adam rose and went to the washroom, he returned to find her awake and waiting for him. She wrapped her arms around him and rocked him as tightly as the seats permitted.

When she released him, it was to give him a look as strong as any he had ever received. One that shaped the words long before she spoke them. Adam was nodding agreement, at least inside himself, before the first hesitant words emerged. Even so, he waited until she was finished to respond with one word. Yes. Then he refitted himself into her arms. And remained like that through the rest of the flight.

They landed at Baltimore/Washington International Airport at midnight according to his body clock. Customs and baggage claim took another hour and a half. They took a taxi to the Days Inn in Crofton. The city was not really a community with definable borders. Washington's dangerous northeastern sprawl infected it from one side, Annapolis wealth from the other. His mother had used it as a base because it let her take pictures in two markets.

The motel receptionist was a friend named Faye. The motel was equidistant from the cancer clinic where his mother had been treated and the hospice where she now resided. The motel sheltered a lot of people in for treatment, or receiving unwanted news, or relatives waiting out the hard hours. Faye showed him her normal grand smile and took a firm hold of his hand. "Now ain't this nice. You finally brought a lady to meet your momma."

"Faye, this is Kayla."

She offered her other pale-palmed hand. "How you doing, girl?"

"Tired but fine."

"Faye's sister is chief nurse at the hospice," Adam explained.

"Yeah, Yolanda thinks the world of his momma. And this boy here. Did Adam tell you about his momma asking him to fly off to England?"

"He did, yes."

"Him going because his momma asked takes first prize in my book." She patted Adam's hand. "It's good you and this fine-looking lady of yours made it back."

"You've heard something?"

"Same as what you've been ready to hear for some time now."

"I talked to her . . ." He struggled to sort through the mental timeline. "Day before yesterday. She sounded fine."

"She *is* fine." Her grip was warm as a heart's fire. "Her Christmas is gonna be spent next to the reason for the season. How much finer can she be?"

The hospice occupied a corner position one street off the main thoroughfare, across a parking lot from Crofton's largest church. The steeple was lit up with Christmas lights, and a Nativity scene was illuminated on the church's front lawn. The hospice's only sign of the season was a tiny tree on the receptionist's desk. Otherwise the front room was the same as always. The outside clock held no importance here. People came when they wanted and stayed as long as they liked. The visitors in the front room each occupied a private space. Their closeness only intensified the respect others showed. The duty nurse hugged Adam as he entered, then gave Kayla the same treatment as soon as they were introduced. One of the hospice's few rules was people fed on hugs long after they lost their interest in food.

"Faye called and said you were on your way," the duty nurse told them. "I'll just go make sure your mother is ready."

His mother made as if to push herself to a seated position as they entered the room. It was a gesture that took him straight back. He had walked into so many rooms, gauging how she felt by this movement. Today her arms scarcely had the strength to track down the sides of her covers, much less raise her up.

Ellen Wright's voice was a skeleton of sound. "Now isn't this nice."

"I'll go fetch another chair," the nurse told them.

"Mom, this is Kayla Austin."

"So very nice to meet you, Mrs. Wright."

"Adam has never brought anyone to see me before." Ellen Wright blinked with the slow cadence of one whose every act was measured. She waited as the nurse set down Adam's chair and her son took a seat. When the door closed, she said, "You are very beautiful, and you must call me Ellen. I sent my boy away for his own good, and look what happens."

Adam said, "Faye told us you've had a turn."

"We both knew this was coming." One hand lifted far enough to brush the air. She did not have the time to waste on such matters. Ellen Wright addressed Kayla. "Even after Adam took his apartment in Washington, he lived here. Do you understand what I'm saying?"

Kayla nodded slowly. "You realized Adam had no life except in this room. So you sent him away, hoping he would learn what he needed to in England."

His mother studied Kayla a long time, before looking at her son and saying, "What a lovely young lady."

"We brought a gift for you." Kayla released Adam's hand and fumbled for the case she had been carrying since insisting that Honor drive her by the office before leaving for Heathrow. The case was large and flat and the color of saddle leather. Kayla opened the flap and gingerly drew out a photograph.

Adam recognized it the instant the image came into view. Then he had to blink very hard to keep it in focus. The Eve Arnold photograph was from *The Bible*, directed by John Huston, who had also played Noah. The picture was of Huston readying himself for one of the shots of the animals on the boat. Huston prepared not by studying his lines, but rather by feeding the animals. He was dressed in a sackcloth robe tied with a rope belt. The animal trainers and the cast all stood and gawked at this great man, kneeling in the dirt and feeding the geese by hand. His mother had hung the same photograph in the hall between their living room and kitchen.

"How lovely," Ellen Wright murmured. "It's always been one of my favorites."

Kayla said, "My mother went through a number of passions in her life. Eve Arnold was one of them."

"You lost your mother?"

Kayla settled the picture on the foot of the bed and used folds in the blanket to prop it open. "When I was thirteen."

Adam looked from the photograph to Kayla and from her to his mother. The two of them chatted with the ease of old friends, or people who had so much in common the words were secondary.

His mother asked, "What was it we were discussing?"

Kayla settled her free hand on top of Ellen's. "You sent Adam away."

"I was becoming increasingly occupied with the other side. Adam needed to see beyond this bed and the coming end. I needed him to see that his struggle was not futile. That it wasn't about my passage. It never has been."

Kayla said, "I don't think I could ever be that brave. Not in a hundred thousand years."

Ellen studied the younger woman. "The joy lies in the struggle. The struggle lies in daring to hope."

Kayla shivered. "Even when it's hopeless?"

"Child, it is never that. Your *reason* for hope changes. Mine has simply gone from the temporary to the eternal." Ellen turned to her son and said, "There is a giant inside you, just waiting to be awakened."

Kayla said it then. Voicing for the very first time what he had agreed to. "Adam has agreed to travel back to Africa with me."

Ellen's gaze tracked back and forth between them. She repeated, "Africa?"

"Tanzania, Mom. Dar es Salaam."

Kayla explained what her project sought to do, the money she hoped to be receiving, the need she had to expand in proper fashion. Nothing so insignificant as a thief and a breaker of dreams. Not in the face of new dreams to take their place. She finished, "I've asked Adam if he would mind coming down and helping me put together a real business plan."

"What about your job in England?"

Kayla's gaze rested on him. "We're only talking about a temporary assignment. One that won't pay much."

"I was a tough bargainer," Adam said. "I held out for a plane ticket and meals."

"He can go back to Daddy in a month or so," Kayla said.

"Maybe," Adam said.

"Yes," Kayla said. "Maybe."

Adam realized his mother was tiring by how her eyes began drifting shut. Though she said nothing, Adam knew it was approaching time to leave. But there was one thing more that needed doing.

He took a long breath, leaned forward, and asked, "I was wondering, Mom. Would you like to pray with me?"

Softly Kayla corrected, "With us."

They found a restaurant catering to the hospital crowd, and a waitress who found nothing out of the ordinary in serving breakfast at eight in the evening. Afterward, Adam drove the rental car back to the motel. Kayla insisted on accompanying him to his room. He stretched out on top of the covers, and Kayla sat down beside him. Adam stared up into her face and saw the love. The calm. The sympathy. The sorrow.

Adam wrapped both his hands about hers. "Thank you."

She leaned over until her forehead touched his own. "You are a good son and a better man, Adam Wright."

He felt his muscles relax one by one. He took in the smell of her hair. He nestled into the fold where her neck met her shoulder. He rubbed his head back and forth and felt her perfume become imbedded into his own skin. She ran her fingers into the hair at the base of his neck. Stroking him as she might a kitten.

He closed his eyes. He slept.

He dreamed he was back standing on the crest of an old man mountain. A gray watchtower rose to his left. A river the color of slate meandered through the valley below. A wind that might have been cold blew against his face and did not touch him at all.

He raised his hands to a rising sun. And he gave thanks with a full heart.

Despite the cloud of sorrow hovering just beyond the horizon, one that was not hidden even inside his dream, Adam realized that here and now, in this miraculous moment, he knew an emotion so powerful it could only be called joy.

A HUSBAND trying to honor his dying wife's last wish

A SEARCH to find the secrets of an ancient estate

BRIAN has the chance to start over . . .

Available at Bookstores Everywhere

THOMAS NELSON
Since 1798

For other products and live events,
visit us at: thomasnelson.com

THE BOOK OF HOURS

Brian Blackstone griped the banister and eased himself down the left-hand set of stairs. The steps' creaking bounced back and forth through the vast formal hall. This one room, the entrance hall to what had once been a splendid English manor, was half the size of his former house. The railing shook and rattled beneath his hands like ill-fitting dentures. But his weakened state forced him to lean heavily on the banister. Each step groaned as if it was ready to break and pitch him headlong. When he reached the stone landing, he heaved a sigh of relief. He heard sounds emanating from the downstairs apartment and hurried for the front door. He needed to meet whoever shared this house, but not now. One thing at a time. It was a creed that had served him well for the past two years.

Outside the solid-oak door, Brian almost stumbled over his valises. The leather suitcases were battered and grimy from two hard years of third-class travel. He had left them there the previous night because he had not felt able to carry them up the winding stairs.And the taxi driver who had brought him in from London's Heathrow Airport had certainly not been willing to take them anywhere, not after he had seen the paltry tip Brian had offered. Brian really was in no shape financially to take a taxi at all. But so late at night there had been no other way to journey from the airport to the village of Knightsbridge.

Brian heaved one case and then the other into the foyer. He unlatched the clasps and dragged out two cotton sweaters and his only jacket. They were the warmest things he owned. The clothes felt distinctly odd, particularly when layered one on top of the other. It was the first time in eleven months he had worn more than sandals, shorts, and a thin cotton shirt.

The December wind made up in wet chill for what it lacked in strength. Brian walked down the graveled drive, sheltered beneath the tallest elms and chestnut trees he had ever seen. Leaves rushed about his feet as the empty branches hummed and rattled overhead. To his right stood a converted stable, red-brick and crumbling. The gatehouse and the manor's main entrance rose just beyond. The entry's tall stone pillars supported a pair of rampant lions clasping some long-forgotten family shield. The iron gates were a full fifty feet wide and thirty high, now rusted permanently open and sagging with age.

The gatehouse was as derelict as the stables. The entire facade was covered in vines, their bases as thick as his thighs where they emerged from the earth. They framed the big lead-paned windows and the doorway. The metal plate set above the mail slot announced that the house was called Rose Cottage.

As he passed through the main gates, he could not help but glance back. His first genuine view of the manor rising above the chestnuts was astonishing. No photograph could possibly do the estate justice, and upon his arrival the house had been reduced by the night and his fatigue to a hulking shadow. Now not even the gray wintry day could erase its decaying grandeur. The house only had three stories, but the ground and second floors were both more than twenty feet high. The Cotswold-stone manor was nine windows broad, and each window measured five feet across.

As he walked the narrow village lane, Brian found himself thinking back to what the taxi driver had said about Knightsbridge. Strange that the man's words seemed clearer now than they had the night before, when the world had drifted vaguely through the mist of Brian's exhaustion. Now, as he walked past brick-and-flint walls bowed with the pressure of uncounted centuries, he heard the man's voice anew. The taxi driver had related how the village was the oldest borough in England. Knightsbridge had been the first capital of William the Conqueror; the ruins of his castle still stood within the village green. The present bridge was erected upon stones set in place by the Romans themselves. The village was filled with centuries of rumors about knights and clandestine monasteries and hidden secrets and mysteriously vanished treasures. On and on the taxi driver had prattled, while Brian huddled in the dark backseat and struggled not to groan.

He felt better after a night's sleep, but slightly feverish and still very weak. The smell of freshly baked bread was the first sign that he was approaching the village's heart. The lane opened into a central square, where a banner announced the annual Christmas market. The plaza was filled with stalls and chatter and people, and flanked by buildings as old as the manor. The chilly air was spiced with mulled cider and cinnamon and cloves. Brian followed his nose to a stall with a rainbow-bright awning and a portable stove displaying trays of hot-cross buns. He pointed and asked, "How much for one of those?"

"Fifty pence, love, and a better bargain you won't be finding here today."

Fifty pence was eighty American cents, too much for a raisin bun as far as he was concerned. But his sense of prices had been seriously distorted by all the places he had recently left behind, and his stomach clenched with hollow hunger. It had been quite a while since he had felt much appetite for anything. "I'll take one, please."

He stepped to the corner of the stall and stood tearing off tiny fragments of the hot bun. Experience had taught him it was far safer to take solid food in small segments. He finished the bun, wiped his sugar-coated hands on his trousers, and waited to see how his stomach responded. When all appeared calm, he returned to the stall's front. "I'll have another, please."

"Knew you would." The woman was as broad as her stall, and the morning's heat caused her to glisten like the buns she sold. "Grand fellow like you couldn't get by on just one."

Brian handed over his money, trying not to wince at the cost, and asked, "Could you tell me where I'd find the Whitehorse Realty Company?"

"Just behind you, love. No, over there, by the solicitors."

Brian thanked the woman and moved back to the side, where the booth blocked the worst of the wind. The day was probably not too cold for early December in England. He had never been in England before. In fact, he had spent two full years avoiding this very arrival.

He felt eyes on him, and knew it was not just his imagination. He tried to remind himself that eyes had followed him through many of his travels, for he had been in a number of places where white men were an oddity. But he could not fool himself into thinking that it did not matter. Here was different. Here he was supposed to feel at home.

A strident shouting match across the square caught his attention. He could not make out the words, but the banners above the two opposing camps were clear enough. Two elderly ladies staffed a narrow stall whose banner read, "Buy a raffle ticket and save the heritage of our village bells." Two hefty women shouted at them and gestured angrily, waving placards as though wishing they were holding battleaxes.

Brian squinted and made out the placard's words: "Ban the noise; ban the bells. Sign our petition today." Just as the argument threatened to come to blows, a lean, middle-aged gentleman wearing a vicar's collar rushed up and swiftly stilled both sides. Brian found himself admiring the man and his ability to calm waters with a few quiet words.

[To continue the story,
please visit your local bookseller.]